TROUBLE VALLEY

TROUBLE VALLEY

Louis Trimble

GUNSMOKE

First published in the UK by Ace Books

This hardback edition 2011
by AudioGO Ltd
by arrangement with
Golden West Literary Agency

ISBN 978 1 445 85647 6

British Library Cataloguing in Publication Data available.

Printed and bound in Great Britain by
CPI Antony Rowe, Chippenham and Eastbourne

I

KIRK GANNON laid down the diamond drill and heavy hammer, and straightened up to take the kinks out of his back. He moved well away from the open box of dynamite before filling and lighting his pipe.

Holding the pipe in his fingers, he let his gaze move slowly along the two timbered slopes which cupped the meadow. The slopes joined at the south to form the hills fronting Snowy Peak; on the north, they dropped suddenly toward the floor of Snowy Valley. Between them on the north, cutting the meadow from the valley, was the high rock wall Kirk had been working on with the drill.

He moved along the ledge of stone that followed the inner side of the wall. A great boulder, washed down to the wall by some long-forgotten flood, gave him a place to sit while he listened. Stilling his breath, he let sounds flow around him. He was seeking something out of place to explain the feeling that had caused him to stop working moments ago. But he could hear only the soft murmur of Snowy Creek's main channel in the middle of the meadow, the lazy hum of insects in the thick marsh grass, the echo of metal on metal as a cowhand worked at the forge on the B-Bar Ranch at this end of the valley. Kirk's roan horse, staked on grassy, dry ground between the edge of the marshy meadow and the beginning of the west slope, grazed peacefully.

"My imagination," Kirk said aloud, but his voice sounded unconvincing even to his own ears. He found his pipe had gone out and he relit it slowly, enjoying the feel of the warm, late-spring air and the sight of Snowy Peak looming large and white-topped. He studied the long fingers of snow running down the scarred mountain face and tried to judge how much water their melt would give in the coming summer.

A sudden nicker from the roan brought Kirk's head around. The horse was looking up the slope to the northwest. Kirk climbed quickly to the rough, notched top of the boulder and followed the roan's gaze. At first he could see nothing, there was only the quick hammering of hoofs on the dry trail. Then a horse and rider came over the crest of the slope and raced toward him. The big, golden horse ran with mane flying. A light touch from the rider brought it to a pawing stop at the edge of the marsh.

Kirk nodded in recognition that the feeling hadn't been his imagination and he let his hands fall away from the gun he had automatically reached for. "You're in an all-fired hurry to paint the mountain today, Arty," he observed.

Arthur Fancher stayed in the saddle, looking down at Kirk without his usual smile of greeting on his blond-bearded face. He was young, and the seriousness of his expression made him seem even more youthful.

"I didn't come to paint today," he blurted out. "I came to warn you. Lex is on his way here—to run you out of the valley."

"And if I don't pack up and get, what then?"

Fancher frowned at Kirk's calm tone. "Then he's going to turn Weeb loose on you."

"Both Lex Cowley and Weeb have been threatening to run me off ever since I came back here last month," Kirk observed. "I can't see that one more threat means much."

Fancher shook his head impatiently. "This is different," he said. "Lex came up here early this morning to see how far along you were with building the dam." He pointed a gloved finger toward the rock wall. "He didn't realize just how close you were to controlling Snowy Creek's flow until he saw for himself."

"And now he's all excited?"

"It's nothing to make light of!" Fancher cried. "After he got back to the ranch, he called Weeb in for a talk. I over-

6

heard them by accident. I only listened because I caught your name.

"I heard Lex say, 'We have to get rid of Gannon before he changes the course of the creek. Once he gets the dam in and working, it'll be too late. That means we act now.' " Fancher's voice trembled. "Then Lex said, 'Gannon has a box of dynamite up there—use it!' "

"I know that trick," Kirk said. "I get blown up with my own powder—only it's made to look like an accident."

"That's what Weeb said! And he sounded as if he'd enjoy killing you."

"There's nothing Weeb would enjoy more," Kirk agreed. "He made that clear when I was dragged out of Snowy Valley ten years ago. He hasn't changed his mind since I came back."

He studied the still excited boy. "We've become pretty good friends since you started coming here to paint," Kirk said. "But Lex Cowley is your stepfather, a man you owe something to. You owe me nothing."

Fancher leaned forward, his hands gripping the saddle horn. "Except for that one year away at art school, I've lived with Lex nine years—since I was thirteen. In the eight years I've spent here in Snowy Valley, I've heard and seen things I knew I wasn't supposed to hear and see. But I always shut my mind to them. I suppose because from the time Lex married my mother and brought us here, he was good to her—and to me. Even after she died, he kept me around, encouraged my painting, even sent me off to school. I guess I shut my mind to the kind of man I knew he really was."

"But today something opened your mind?" Kirk asked quietly.

Fancher flushed under his thin beard. "After Lex and Weeb got through talking about you, Lex started in on Carla Belden—about getting the B-Bar Ranch away from

7

her this summer." Anger shook his voice. "You know how Lex talks when his impatience gets the best of him; that's the way he was this morning. He told Weeb he'd better not make any more mistakes and that if he didn't fix it so you couldn't help Carla get water for the B-Bar, he'd have to depend on me to do the job."

"On you?" Kirk echoed. "What the devil did he man by that?"

"I didn't understand at first," Fancher admitted. "But then Weeb made some coarse jokes, and I figured it out. Lex has known for years that Carla was to inherit Sam Belden's ranch when he died and—and he's kept me around figuring to use me. Now I understand why Lex made sure Carla and I saw a lot of each other when she came last year, and why he's been so eager to have us get married. He thinks that once she's my wife and I control the B-Bar, I'll sell to him without a fight."

"If he's so sure, why should he bother with me?" Kirk wondered. "All he has to do is wait until you two get married this fall."

"He isn't that sure," Fancher said bitterly. "I heard him tell Weeb, 'We have to make sure. I can't trust that fool kid not to do something so Carla won't marry him, or not to go noble after they are married, and make me fight him to get the B-Bar. That means we do what we have to now.' "

"Would you have fought him?"

Fancher looked away. "What have I got to fight with?" he demanded. He held out his hands to Kirk. "These? They're fine for holding a paint brush. But they're useless with a gun. I'm just not the kind to fight the way Lex fights— getting what he wants any way he has to—any dirty way!"

Kirk said gently, "When I was hauled away from the valley ten years ago, it was because I knew what kind Cowley was and I thought I could fight him—his way." He grinned sourly. "Smarter people than I was knew that a nineteen-year-old didn't stand a chance against Cowley or Weeb, so they got my relatives to take me away after my father was killed."

He nodded at Fancher. "But in those ten years I've learned a lot, I think. I've run into other men like Cowley—and I've fought my share of them. They're all the same—hungry for land, for power, for what being rich can bring them. And they don't care who they trample to get what they want."

He paused and added, "And you're no more equipped to fight that kind of man than I am to paint a picture of your horse." He would have said more but a distant sound caught his attention. He stood listening.

"Horse coming," he said shortly. "You ride out of here fast." He saw the doubt on Arthur Fancher's features and added, "Don't worry, I'm not going after Cowley with a gun. Not unless he starts something first. And you can bet he won't. Your stepfather doesn't do his own dirty work as long as he can find someone else to do it for him."

Fancher said with bitter despair, "I wish I'd never learned these things about Lex." Reining the gold around, he sent it hurtling up the slope and into the timber.

Kirk went back to the big rock, relit his cold pipe, and waited. He could hear a horse coming steadily up the trail that led from the southwest corner of the valley.

He expected Lex Cowley, and he wasn't disappointed. In a few minutes, a leggy, white horse appeared. The man in the fancy saddle was big, with strong features, his hair beginning to silver at the temples. He reined up part way down the slope and, with the arrogance of complete self-assurance, stared at Kirk.

"You're wasting a lot of time and effort, Gannon," he said. "I don't want that dam finished."

Kirk grinned easily. "Tell Carla Belden, not me. This is her land; I just work for her." His grin broadened at Cowley's unyielding expression. "Despite what you keep thinking, I didn't come here to push you or your so-called cowhands around for what happened in the past. You aren't worth the effort. I came because of a chance to rebuild the valley land you and others like you have let go to hell these last years."

Cowley said thinly, "Before you left here, you ran around blaming me for everything that happened—including your father's death in that stampede. Now you're blaming me for the years of drought."

"You're a lot of things," Kirk answered, "but being a fool isn't one of them, Cowley. You knew what would happen when you ran sheep on cattle pasture gone dry for want of rain. But you did it. Oh, not on your own land. On land you leased—so that when it got in bad enough shape, you could buy it for next to nothing."

"Who told you that old wives' tale, that fool Ira Moss?"

"I checked the land records at the county seat before I came back here," Kirk said. "They told me who leased what and when, and who bought what and when." He waved it aside with a quick gesture. "But Ira did tell me that between the time Sam Belden died and Carla came from Wyoming to live here, your stock broke through fencing and nearly ruined half of the B-Bar's hay land—the best half."

"I didn't come here to listen to your windy talk," Cowley said. "I came to tell you to ride out."

"I have a contract to fill," Kirk said evenly. "When that's done, then I'll make up my mind whether to move on or stay."

"You'll leave—today!" Cowley snapped. He made an obvious effort and caught up the unraveling threads of his impatience. "Don't forget, Gannon, I'm a lot more around here than I was ten years ago. I own a good piece of the valley now. And what I don't own, I control—or will soon."

He leaned forward, a cold smile on his flat, harsh mouth. "Before I'm done I'll have everything, and the town along with it."

Cowley was sure of himself, Kirk thought. He wouldn't have boasted so openly this way if he hadn't been certain that sundown would find Kirk hightailing it north to Riverport and Washington Territory on the other side of the Columbia River.

Kirk stood up and thumbed his hat back from his forehead. "You've made a pretty good try at running me out already, Cowley. You've got most of the businessmen scared to sell me the supplies I need. You've got old Marshal Downes threatening to chase me away if I spit in his street—" He broke off and let his smile mock Cowley. "But take a good, close look. All the time you've been trying to have me rousted out of here, I've been working. And as soon as I reroute Snowy Creek through the wall there so that half of it doesn't disappear underground in porous rock, I'll be about finished. All I'll need then is a control gate—and then there'll be a lake filling this meadow. After that when folks want to grow hay, they'll have the water they need. They can stop selling off their stock cheap to you every time a dry year comes along."

He widened his smile. "A meadow filled with water in less than two weeks, Cowley."

"In two weeks you'll be worm food," Cowley snapped. "I control this valley, Gannon; it's mine! I've worked fifteen years here to get what I want. And no homemade-dam builder is going to stop me. You ride out of my country today or get carried out in a box tomorrow."

He reined his big horse around and started up the slope. Kirk called out in soft mockery, "Have you told Carla and Arty yet that you want them married so you can get her ranch away from her? That you couldn't get anywhere

11

fighting old Sam Belden for it, and you haven't done much better against his niece?"

Kirk saw Cowley's impatience rise up as he swung in the saddle, his jaw muscles twitching in an effort to control himself. He turned back abruptly and sent the white horse up the slope and out of sight.

Kirk let his grin slip away. He had learned ten years ago that Lex Cowley never made idle threats. That meant Weeb and some of his crew of hard cases would be along as soon, Kirk guessed, as Cowley got to town where he could be seen by witnesses. Kirk knew if anything happened to him, not only Cowley but Weeb and the other L-in-C men would have proof they were somewhere else when the trouble came.

Kirk grunted as a thought washed across his mind. If he did manage to stay and finish the dam, what then? Once Cowley got Carla Belden's land from her, he—Cowley—would be the one to gain from the water. He'd have control of it and, unlike any other valley ranchers, he would use that control to gain more power.

Kirk swore. Not only would Cowley control the water from Snowy Creek once he had control of the B-Bar, he would also control the only trail that led into the summer grass in the east hills. No man would be able to call himself his own boss from that time on.

Kirk looked up at the blue sky and the towering, white mountain. His grin came back, a little bitter now. He had come home hoping to set to rights the badly abused land, and it had seemed a simple thing once he'd talked Carla into letting him dam the meadow. But now it was something else.

Ten years ago he'd wanted to stay and fight Cowley, he thought. Now he had the chance, but it meant fighting the marshal and most of the town's businessmen and a good many of the ranchers—all indebted one way or another to

Lex Cowley. It also meant finding a way to protect Carla Belden and to put some fighting ability into Arty Fancher's hands.

Quietly, Kirk drew his gun and checked it. It wouldn't be long before Weeb and his professional gunmen showed up. Almost idly, Kirk wondered how many he would bring along to help him fight one man.

II

Weeb will bring as many men as he thinks he needs to get the job done, Kirk thought. *He's not one to waste manpower.* Kirk looked around, studying the slopes rising on either side of the meadow. The L-in-C men would come over their crests, at least one on each side. The rock wall blocked him to the north, the clinging mud of the marsh to the south.

Kirk nodded. Weeb would try to box him in. Unless he rode out, he would have to let himself be boxed.

He moved quickly now, not sure how much time he had left. Getting his carbine from his saddle boot, he carried it to the big rock and wedged the barrel in one of the notches at the top so that the muzzle was aimed at a patch of shade on the west slope. He ran a heavy cord from the trigger, laying the free end on the meadow side of the rock.

That done, he fused three sticks of dynamite carefully and put them upright in his shirt pocket. Knocking out his pipe, he refilled it and put it away for later use. Then he sat on the rock and waited.

He could hear them before they topped the rise of the west slope—two horses moving steadily over the hard-packed trail. Kirk turned his attention eastward, across the marsh to the slope of that side. There the timber was thicker with more underbrush between the deep-ridged boles of the ponderosas. He was seeking movement, some sign of

Weeb's man on that side. But nothing moved in that direction.

The sound of the horses had stopped. Kirk cocked his head, listening in the silence. He caught the faint sound of a tiny twig cracking under a boot sole. An angry voice whispered a shushing sound. There were two of them on foot now, Kirk guessed. It was probably Weeb and his shadow, Opie. Where Weeb went, Opie went, too. The latter was a small, ferretlike parasite living on the big man's strength. He repaid Weeb for his protection by lying for him and sometimes by killing for him.

Kirk took a moment to light his pipe. Making sure it was drawing well, he rose and strolled to the edge of the rock, leaning on it near the point where the cord attached to the trigger of his carbine dangled. From here he could see most of the west slope.

At first his eyes picked out only shadows. Then one split into two and Kirk could see Weeb's bearish body and Opie's small, darting form. Opie was easing slowly south away from Weeb and working so as to get an angle on the big rock.

Kirk called pleasantly, "Hold it right there, both of you." He caught the cord, shielding his hand from the two men with his body.

Opie froze. Weeb made a quick move and sunlight glinted from the barrel of his handgun. Kirk called, "Throw it down, Weeb. I'm not alone here."

"The devil you ain't," Weeb shouted back in his rough voice. "Ira Moss went to town early with the freight wagon, and who else in these parts is fool enough to side with you against the L-in-C?"

Kirk twitched the cord. The carbine barked, spraying dirt not far from where Weeb stood. At the same instant, Kirk leaped behind the protection of the boulder.

"By God!" Opie cried shrilly. "He ain't alone."

"Who the devil's there with him?" Weeb demanded.

His voice rose to a shout. "Bingo, who's over there with Gannon?"

Kirk grinned. He had learned what he wanted to know. At least one man was on the east slope. He moved swiftly, sliding along the boulder, his face turned to the east. He caught a blur of movement as a lanky man came out of shadow and into position for a shot across the front of the meadow.

"I can't see nobody but Gannon," he called in a reedy voice.

"Drive him out this way!" Weeb ordered.

Bingo's gun came up and he fired. Kirk was moving and the lead whined off rock to his right. As he danced into shadow, he drew his own .44. Another shot probed for him, sending rock spitting from the top of the boulder. Kirk answered, firing from the hip. He aimed for Bingo's gun arm. Bingo cried out and jerked forward, stumbling on the burshy slope. Kirk shot again, aiming for a leg now. Bingo cursed in shrill pain and tumbled down, rolling until he lay half on dry land and half in the marsh. He kept up a steady stream of cursing as he tried to haul himself out of the muck and failed.

"Bingo won't be much help from now on," Kirk called to Weeb. He pulled the carbine out of its notch and put his eye there. Opie was sidling along the slope again. There were ten feet between him and Weeb.

Kirk called, "I told you both to hold it."

"This won't do you no good," Weeb shouted. "I can bring a dozen men if I have to. So don't make it harder on yourself than you have to, Gannon. We come to give you a chance to ride out. A smart man takes the best deal he can get—so be smart."

"Bring a dozen men," Kirk answered. "I've got a box of dynamite—the dynamite you figured on using on me. Bring your men and I'll show you and them how to handle it." He paused and added, "I have three sticks primed right now."

Weeb said thickly, "We come here peaceable, Gannon, and you started shooting us up. The marshal will have something to say about that!"

Kirk chuckled. Weeb hadn't liked the remark about the dynamite, so now he was going to try to use the law for his hole card.

"Weeb," Kirk called in a light voice, "before you go to see Marshal Downes you'd better pack Bingo off to the hospital. From the way he's caterwauling, he sounds like he needs a little help."

"I'm giving you one last chance to ride!" Weeb cried.

Kirk laid the barrel of his gun in the notch at the top of the boulder, took deliberate aim and fired. Dirt spurted near Weeb's feet, making him leap.

"Let me see your guns hit the ground," Kirk snapped. "I've got too much work to do to fool around with you all day. Now move!"

Two guns dropped to the dirt. Kirk said, "Now get over there and pick up Bingo. He's about ready for Doc Irmser."

Weeb turned and started up the slope; Opie hesitated and then followed. Kirk snapped, "The short way is across the meadow. Take it."

Weeb hesitated, cursing. But another bullet close to his boots sent him striding down the slope. Opie came behind, staying well back as if distance from Weeb might protect him. When they reached the meadow, both paused. Kirk came into the open, waggling his gun. Cursing, Weeb plunged into the reed-filled soil. Opie tried to say where he was but a word from Kirk sent him after the big man.

Boots slobbered as they lifted from the muck. Once Opie left a boot behind and had to stop to retrieve it. When they reached the middle of the meadow, they went knee deep in the cold water of the creek's main channel. Weeb was panting and swearing at the same time as he finally staggered onto dry land.

"Now pack Bingo back here," Kirk called. "You, Opie, pick up Bingo's gun and empty it. And let me see four shells flying out into the meadow."

Opie did as he was told. Then taking Bingo's legs and leaving the heavier shoulders for Weeb, he followed his protector back across the swampy marsh. As they walked, Kirk went up the slope and emptied their guns. When they staggered past, muck-covered well above their knees, he pushed Weeb's gun into its holster and Opie's into his waistband. Then he looked down at the bony features of Bingo and wondered how long it would be before the killer came after him, looking for revenge.

"I ain't forgetting this—any of it," Weeb growled.

"I wouldn't want you to," Kirk said evenly. "And I wouldn't want you to miss telling Cowley that he's started something he might have trouble finishing."

Weeb paused in his stride and glowered at Kirk. "What the devil is that supposed to mean?"

"I didn't start pushing," Kirk answered. "Cowley did. He —and you too—seemed to think I was still a wet-eared kid who doesn't know how to push back. That was your mistake."

"You threatening us, Gannon?"

Kirk studied the burly body and the heavy, sour features. "Put it his way," he said. "Tell Cowley to stop pushing me and I'll stop pushing back. Tell him to be satisfied with what he's stolen over the years and leave the B-Bar and the rest of the valley alone."

Weeb seemed about to answer. Then he turned and moved on, still carrying the heavy end of the burden. At the crest of the slope, he looked back. "You'll be out of Snowy Valley before morning, Gannon. I ain't going to tell you again."

17

Kirk remained where he was, watching Weeb lead the way over the crest and out of sight. He guessed Bingo would be packed on Opie's horse around to where his own was tied. Then Weeb would take Bingo to the doctor in town. He was too valuable a man—too deadly with a gun—to risk losing.

Kirk thought of the boldness of his words to Weeb and smiled sourly. Cowley had a dozen men on his payroll, and he could get a dozen more from the mines and hill ranches at the northeast corner of the valley. Excepting Ira Moss, Kirk couldn't think of any man who would be sure to side with him. That made it two against two dozen.

"And those aren't much in the way of odds," he observed aloud. Going back to where he had been working on the rock wall, he defused the dynamite, put the sticks back in the box, and then went to his grazing roan. Mounting, he sent the horse up the west slope and onto the hill trail that wound above the west side of the valley to the town of Snowy.

He paused at the edge of a small creek. This was the boundary between Ira Moss' Oval-M and Carla Belden's B-Bar. Near him was a trail that bent down to the valley to meet the wagon road to town. He thought about taking the wagon road and decided against it. Even with the hills and turns on the trail, Kirk knew he could make better time than by using the easier but longer valley road. Putting the roan across the creek, he cantered down the trail.

He was near the trail leading left to Ira's small ranch house when a horse and rider burst from the timber. Kirk slapped a hand to his gun and then straightened up, grunting. It was Fancher on his gold horse.

"This is no time to come up suddenly on a man," Kirk snapped.

Fancher said, "Sorry, but I wanted you to know I heard everything that happened when Weeb and Opie and Bingo came to the meadow." He smiled in reluctant admiration. "You were pretty rough on them."

"I intended to be. I want Weeb to know what it's like being on the other end of things for a change," Kirk said.

"Weeb won't forget, and he won't forgive. You've just made more trouble for yourself."

"And I intend to make a little more," Kirk answered. "If I move along, I can reach town before he gets Bingo there. And like a good citizen, I'm going to report the shooting to Marshal Downes."

"What makes you think he'll believe you?"

"Why should he believe Weeb more than he does me?" Kirk demanded. "Cowley doesn't own Downes yet. You look back and you'll see that he's been the main reason Cowley has moved so slowly all these years. Between Downes and Judge Breen, Cowley's had to cover his tracks before he dared make any big move. And today he made a mistake. He got impatient. I'm going to make some hay out of that mistake if I can."

He started on. Fancher trotted his horse alongside the roan. "Lex will have himself covered for today too," he said. He ran a gloved hand over his face. "When I think of all the things I heard over the years—and refused to understand."

"You've quit refusing," Kirck said almost gently. "It isn't easy, but it's something you have to face up to."

"But what can I do?" Fancher cried. "You know how much the B-Bar means to Carla—and how much she means to me. For the first time in her life, she has something she feels is her own, that she knows won't disappear out from under her overnight."

Kirk shook his head. "All I know about Carla is that she's young and mighty pretty and good at running a ranch. I met her a few times when I was a kid and she visited Sam at the B-Bar. But she was a little girl, nothing anyone ten years older would pay attention to. All I remember is that she lived somewhere in Wyoming with her father."

"They lived in a lot of Wyoming," Fancher said with soft bitterness. "Her father never would admit he'd been sent away from England by his family. He spent his life trying to live like an English gentleman—dressing every night for dinner, spending his money on fancy foolishness, sending Carla away to a finishing school—all to impress the English managers of those big cattle ranches. Carla never knew from one year to the next where she'd be. Her father was always selling, claiming the next place was better and would make them rich.

"And when she came to the B-Bar last year, she finally had something of her own—as bad a shape as it was in after what Lex did to it in the year between then and the time Sam died. That ranch has become a part of her, Kirk. I can't just stand by and let Lex take it way from her."

"Damn it, man. Then fight for it—for her."

"How?" Fancher cried. "Do I shoot Lex? The only time I ever handled a gun I nearly shot myself in the leg." He looked very young, very conscious of his own inadequacies.

"Fight the way you know how—with your brains. Lex Cowley's a smart man, but it's the kind of smartness a fox has. And he never considers anything except by the way it's going to affect him. You've got a better brain than that. Use it!"

Fancher stared at him. "You're the first person who ever even let me think I could do anything but paint pictures," he said.

They rode in silence for some distance. Kirk spoke first, pointing to a trail slanting off to the right. "Here's where you turn off," he said. "The next trail goes down to the edge of town."

"That's where I'm going," Fancher said. "To town."

His stiff tone of voice caught Kirk's attention. "I don't need a bodyguard," he said softly.

"No, but you need someone to back up your story against Weeb," Fancher said flatly. "And I'm the only one who can do that."

Kirk reined in and stared at him. "Now who's making trouble for himself?"

"You told me to fight the way I know how. One of the ways is with words," Fancher answered. Heeling the gold, he sent it spurting along the trail, forcing the roan to work to keep up.

III

SHORTLY BEFORE they reached town, Kirk glimpsed a trio of riders below and to the south on the valley road. "That'll be Weeb," he said. "We've got a good fifteen minutes on them."

A short distance on, they came to the top of Snowy's main cross street. They rode past the fancier homes and Doc Irmser's sprawling house with its single-room hospital, turned into the alley running behind the bank, and went to the rear of the jail. Leaving their horses at the hitching rail there, they went inside.

Marshal Downes was at his deak studying a sheaf of circulars. He looked up and nodded. There was no welcome for Kirk in his glance.

"I came to report a shooting," Kirk said. He sat down and sketched out what had happened.

Downes' aging features settled into a frown. "And you say that Weeb is on his way here?"

"With a different story, most likely," Kirk answered.

"Kirk's is the right one," Fancher said. "I saw and heard the whole thing."

21

Downes swung to stare at him with pale-blue eyes. "You're backing Gannon?"

"That's right," Fancher said in a level voice.

Downes thumbed back his hat and reached for a sheet of paper. "I'll take down your statements," he said. "You bringing charges, Gannon?"

"No charges," Kirk said. "I just want to get the record straight."

Downes wet a pen and scratched it slowly across the paper as Kirk repeated what he'd said. When the statement was finished, Kirk signed. The marshal took another sheet but Fancher waved it away. Instead he scrawled under Kirk's signature in bold letters, "I hereby swear that the above statement is true and accurate. I was an eyewitness." He signed his own name with a flourish.

"If I was you," Downes said dryly, "I'd figure on having it rough when I got back to the L-in-C tonight."

"I've thought of that."

Downes shrugged. Before he could say more, the door slammed open and Weeb stalked in. He pulled up short as he saw Kirk and Fancher. "What kind of lies you listening to, Marshal?"

"I've taken Gannon's statement about what happened in the meadow today," Downes said evenly. "I've got Fancher's statement that he was an eyewitness and that he agrees with Gannon. If you want to add something or change it, I'll take that down."

Weeb sucked in his breath and stared at Fancher. "You backed up Gannon?"

"Stop trying to bully me," Fancer said. "You've had fun doing that ever since I came to live with Lex. But it's over—as of today. I heard you and Lex talking this morning."

He rose and faced Weeb. The slender young man's face drained of color as he fought to keep his voice from shaking. "I went to the meadow and warned Kirk of the plan to run him out of the valley. And I stayed and listened to everything that happened."

"Someday I'm going to whip you, you lying pup!" Weeb snarled. He took a threatening step toward Fancher, swinging his heavy shoulders like an angry bear.

Kirk stood up and stepped between them. "Try me instead, Weeb. You used to get a lot of pleasure slapping me around when I was about his age. But I haven't noticed you being so eager since I came back."

"I can still whip you," Weeb growled. "And if you're around tomorrow or after, I'll do it!"

"I'll be here," Kirk said. He mocked Weeb with a grin. "Let's say a week from tonight." His voice was deliberately goading. "Here, in town."

Weeb pushed his face toward Kirk. "If you're here in a week, Gannon, I'll just take you up on that."

Downes snapped, "Break it up, both of you. This is my office, not a saloon. And if you have your fight, see that it's a fair one." His eyes measured Weeb challengingly. "And that doesn't include one between you and young Fancher." He picked up his pen. "You ready to make your statement, Weeb?"

"The devil with it," Weeb growled. "If a man can't get heard when he's got the truth to tell, there ain't no point in wasting his breath." He stomped away.

Kirk turned to Fancher and found him staring out the window. Looking over Fancher's shoulder, Kirk saw that Carla Belden had come to town. She rode sidesaddle, as she always did when she wasn't working on the range. Kirk thought she looked especially appealing in her full riding skirt, fancy shirt, jacket and riding hat.

"Thanks for your help," Kirk said.

Fancher took the hint, said, "My pleasure," and hurried out.

Kirk nodded to Downes and started away. The marshal

said thinly, "Wait a minute, Gannon. Where do you think you're going?"

"Over to Mindy's Palace for some dinner," Kirk answered. "I expect Ira'll be there."

"I know Cowley is," Downes said dryly. "Anyone bothering to look across the street can see his horse."

"If Cowley leaves me alone, I'll leave him alone," Kirk answered. "If he doesn't, I'm not going to sit back and take a rousting—or let him run me out of the valley." He shook his head. "I'm not going to Mindy's to cause trouble. I think too much of her for that."

"Don't you go getting Mindy any more interested in you than she is already," Downes said. "I don't want to see her hurt when you pack up and leave."

"You sound like Cowley and Weeb, Marshal. What makes you think I have any intention of leaving? I came back here because Ira Moss wrote and said that Carla and the valley land needed help. When I first got here and talked her into letting me build the dam, I didn't think much about staying—but it's been in my mind since then."

He studied Downes' inflexible expression. "Marshal, I'm not the wild-eyed kid I was ten years ago. I've lived a lot of places since then, and I've learned a pretty good trade—thanks to that engineer that apprenticed me eight years back. And when I started helping people rebuild their land and get water they needed, I knew I had found the kind of work I wanted to do. And there's a lifetime of it for one man in these parts. So I've decided to live here again—it's the best place to start rebuilding."

"You're being mighty windy," Downes observed. "But words don't change the trouble, and you know it."

"I didn't start it. Cowley did. And you know *that!*"

Downes said persistently, "Since you returned I've felt the trouble building. I've been a lawman too long not to smell that kind of thing. And my nose tells me there's a real storm coming. My job is to stop it before it hits."

"Tell that to Cowley," Kirk said. He took a step toward the desk. "I'm no drifter to be pushed on to the next man's town, Marshal. I'm a substantial citizen with money in my pocket and a job to my hand. Or doesn't that make any difference, when Cowley is the man who wants me away from here?"

Downes flushed. "I don't work for Cowley any more than I ever did."

"No one claims that," Kirk said quietly. "But there are ways of getting a man to do the things you want him to. Cowley has two-thirds of the local businessmen in his palm. Those are the same men who hired you and see you get your wages. They can get you fired, too."

The color drained from Downes' face. His voice was thin. "That's their business," he said. "I do what I think is best for the town and the valley. It's my country too, remember, Gannon. I own my little spread, just as Judge Breen and Lawyer Parker and a lot of other townsmen own theirs. We don't like Cowley's pushing any more than you do. But we don't want a blowup either. That means friends taking sides against each other. I've seen it in other places; I don't want it here."

"So if it comes down to Cowley pushing too hard and my pushing back, I'm the one that gets run out—is that it?"

"What would you do in my place—try to hand-haul a buggy or a freight wagon?"

"If the freight wagon was more in the way, then I'd find me some good horses and pull it aside," Kirk said softly. With a nod he left.

He rode up the alley. Across from the bank was a one-time hotel, now a freshly painted building with a fancy sign over the portico. It proclaimed, *Mindy's Palace.*

Kirk tied his horse at the hitching rail and went through

the wide doors into what had been the lobby of the hotel. To his left, the once huge dining room had been converted into a place for men to come for food and drink and, when traveling shows came, entertainment on the small stage at the back. On the right, the bar had been made into a family dining room, with a side entrance for ladies who wished to come unescorted. Kirk turned to the left.

At this time, the end of the dinner hour, a number of men in town clothes or rancher's clothes occupied most of the tables that filled the middle of the room. Along the front wall was the long, shiny bar with a fancy mirror behind it. *In its way this is a saloon,* Kirk thought. At the same time, it was a place for people to come and relax and have some recreation in a decent atmosphere. For those who preferred the stench of stale liquor and a chance for a good fight, there was Grogarty's a block down the street. If a man found Grogarty's too tame, he could go another block to the Cowman's Bar.

Sipping a glass of beer, Ira Moss was leaning on the mahogany. Mindy herself moved through the room, pausing at various tables to make sure that everything was right or to signal one of her waitresses to bring more water or more bread and butter. Kirk stood and watched her.

She was a tall woman with a fine, bold figure. Her face was nearly beautiful with its high cheekbones hinting at Indian blood and its natural color highlighted by her mass of hair the color of ripened wheat. Her eyes, Kirk had learned that day they'd met a month back, were as smoky a gray as his own, but with flecks of gold dancing in them.

Beyond Mindy, Kirk saw three men taking their ease at a table. He smiled thinly as he moved toward the bar. Cowley was making sure he had solid witnesses to testify he had been in town around noon—Judge Breen and Lawyer Parker. The fact that they obviously tolerated Cowley's presence out of politeness and a desire to keep down the tension in the valley bothered Cowley not at all.

Mindy turned, saw Kirk, and threw him a quick smile. She glanced toward Cowley's table. He had lifted his head and was staring at Kirk, his mouth a thin, tight line. Kirk turned from the bar and strolled toward the table. As he passed Mindy, he said softly, "I don't intend to cause trouble."

"I didn't expect you would. But Cowley looks as if he'd welcome it."

"He's disappointed," Kirk said. "He thinks Weeb ran me out of the valley."

He moved on, stopping at the table to nod at the three men. "Howdy Judge, Mr. Parker. Cowley, I thought you'd like to know one of your men is over in Doc Irmser's hospital." With another nod, he started away.

Judge Breen called him back. "How's the work coming on the dam?" Although he had been elderly when Kirk was a boy, his voice was still strong and vigorous, as was his lean body.

"Another week or so, Judge, and there'll be water for everybody."

"If Carla Belden lets it go," Cowley snapped.

"She never struck me as being greedy," Kirk observed. "She's interested in having successful ranchers for neighbors—like any decent person would be."

Cowley slammed down his napkin and stood up. With a brief nod at his table companions, he strode away. Judge Breen laughed softly. Lawyer Parker settled a smile on his round face. "That was well done, Kirk. If you want a job as my trial lawyer, just say the word."

"I just thought you might enjoy your after-dinner cigar more if you were alone," Kirk said. He went back to the bar and took a place alongside the small, wizened form of Ira Moss.

27

His lined, old face broke into a grin. "Come to town to celebrate getting a hole blown in that rock wall?"

"I didn't get a chance," Kirk said. He glanced around, saw that only Mindy was near them, and briefly outlined what had happened.

"You shot up Bingo!"

"After he took two shots at me," Kirk said.

Mindy said in her husky voice, "And Arty Fancher saw it all—and told the marshal? I didn't know he had that kind of courage."

"Nor did I," Kirk admitted. "But he has, and he'll get more. He learned a lot about himself today when he stood up to Weeb."

He paused and added, "I learned about myself, too. I've decided to stay here after the dam is built."

Mindy's smile slipped. "Have you asked Cowley about that?" she asked bitterly.

"I didn't figure on asking Cowley if I could stay or not," Kirk said. He smiled at her and then became serious, turning to Ira Moss. "If you're still planning on taking the freight wagon to Riverport later in the week, I need some supplies."

Ira said sourly, "Like the ones you tried to get the Mercantile to order last week."

"The same ones the Mercantile refused to ship in for me," Kirk agreed. "Cowley has a pretty good hold on this town," he added.

"Not on me, he doesn't." Mindy bristled. "And he won't have as long as I'm able to lift a gun."

"Cowley ain't anxious to push you, not since you made him look a fool when he tried it before," Ira Moss said. "On the other hand, he don't forgive. If he sees a chance to run you out and cover himself at the same time, he'll take it real quick. Don't you forget it."

He turned to Kirk. "You help me load the wagon, I'll

run it back to the Oval-M now and then give you a hand in the meadow."

"I'd rather you ran the wagon back here after unloading so you could get an early start for those supplies," Kirk said. "I'd go myself but I don't want to leave the dam site too long, and I don't want Cowley to think he's run me out of the valley."

"I don't mind going tomorrow," Ira Moss said. "I got an order to fill for Mindy, too."

Mindy said softly, "You'll be alone at the Oval-M while Ira's gone, Kirk. Sleep with one eye open. The next time you come to town, I wouldn't want it to be crosswise over your saddle."

IV

Fancher put his gold horse alongside Carla's sorrel and looked through the bay window of the dressmaker's shop. He could see her inside, trying a hat on her dark hair. Dismounting, he went inside.

She was nearly twenty—a smiling, attractive girl with the often simple, uncluttered beliefs of youth still on her face and in her dark eyes. Her smile broadened as she saw Fancher, and there was no doubting her affection for him.

"You shouldn't spy on me! I'm trying on hats for our honeymoon."

"Shameless," he teased. "Are you trying to get me to admit in front of witnesses that I'm going to marry you?"

Since the invitations had been printed and sent some time before, Betty Matson, the dressmaker and milliner, allowed herself a giggle. Carla joined her and then began to chatter about clothes. She stopped abruptly. "Arthur, you aren't listening."

"Sorry," he said. "Maybe I'm getting a little scared by it all."

Carla studied him briefly and then, with a word to Betty Matson, put her hand on Fancher's arm and let him escort her out. After Fancher had helped her onto the sorrel and settled in the saddle of the gold, she said quietly, "Something is troubling you, isn't it? Something besides the wedding."

He nodded. "I was in the meadow this morning with Kirk. Lex came and then Weeb and two men followed." He sketched out what had happened, not because he wanted to boast of his own part, but to make sure that she heard the story from him before Lex Cowley could mangle it.

She frowned. "Ira told me the other day that Lex has been trying to get Kirk out of the valley. But why? What Kirk is doing will help everyone!"

"Don't forget that you have the legal right to keep all that water for yourself. You own the headwaters of Snowy Creek."

"Does Lex think I'd do that? He couldn't. He's too—too smart. Surely he understands how things will be with all that water." She took a deep breath. "You must have misunderstood Lex, Arthur. I'm sure that Weeb acted on his own against Kirk. I know they hate one another."

"I'll find out how much I misunderstood when I get home," Fancher said dryly. He rode slowly out of town with her.

Lex Cowley stood at the big front window of the L-in-C ranch house and looked south toward the neighboring B-Bar. Snowy Creek caught the slant of the sun and threw slivers of silver at him. Off to the east, he could see the trail leading to the summer grass, where most of the valley ranchers had their stock at this season.

"Once I get it, I'm in control," he said aloud. He turned

to a waiting Weeb. "Arthur is coming from Carla's place now. That was a fool thing, theatening him in front of the marshal."

"I was pretty mad," Weeb said. "After all you done for the kid—"

"Don't worry about what I've done for him. It's what he's going to do for me that counts. And you leave him to me. I don't want any trouble until the wedding is over and transfer of title is made to me."

Weeb grinned, showing stained teeth. "And then he's mine?"

"And then you can have him," Cowley said shortly.

"What about Gannon? Do I leave him alone too?"

Cowley frowned. "Keep your lip to yourself. I already told you what I want done with Gannon. And this time, do the job right! After the way you ran off at the mouth in front of Downes, you'll have to be careful. He's nobody's fool. So don't take chances. Wait until there's no chance of making a mistake."

He waved a hand. "Get out of here. Arthur's coming in."

Weeb went out, swaggering. In a few minutes Fancher entered the big parlor with his portable easel under his arm and his paint box in his hand. Dropping his equipment, he began to take off his riding gloves. He nodded coolly to Cowley.

"Weeb told me what happened at the marshal's office today," Cowley said.

"I expected him to," Fancher answered. He was surprised to find his voice so steady.

"You'd be smarter if you kept out of things that don't concern you."

"Carla concerns me," Fancher retorted quietly. He had spent a lot of the time working on what he would say to Cowley as he had come from the B-Bar. "When we marry, I'll own a piece of her ranch. That concerns me, too."

31

"If you're talking about Kirk Gannon and his fool dam— if I'd wanted that kind of work, I'd have hired it done."

Fancher scratched his thin, blond beard. "But you know how much the dam will help the valley. So if someone else is paying for what will help you, why should you complain?" He let his lips smile. "After all, to really have control of the valley you'll need that dam and the water rights to Snowy Creek."

Cowley frowned. "You're talking riddles. I don't own the B-Bar; Carla does. In a little while, you will."

"Stop thinking I'm fifteen years old," Fancher said in the same quiet voice. "I'll admit I turned a deaf ear to most of what went on here these years, but today I overheard you and Weeb plotting—and a lot of things began to make sense that didn't before. I know why you're so eager for me to marry Carla."

"You damn little snoop!"

"I overheard by accident," Fancher said, "and I'm thankful I did." He shook his head slowly. "You're confident even now—even after you know how I feel. Because you know I won't fight you—that I can't. I'm not made that way, I guess. Once I've married Carla, you'll make me sell to you."

He moved toward the door. "So I've decided not to marry her. If I did, I'd be betraying her. That ranch is too much a part of her life for me to do that. I'm sorry, Lex, but I won't help you."

Cowley stared at him, a muscle in his jaw twitching as he fought to control himself. Finally he said, "You'll marry her at the time set." He swung away and back. "No, by God! You'll marry her before that. As soon as I can arrange it. Now get to your room and start thinking of a way to talk her into changing the date. It's going to be this coming Sunday."

"You're wasting your breath. I've already made up my

mind," Fancher said. "I'll to to my room, but it'll be to pack. I'm leaving today."

"Don't tell me what you'll do and what you won't do. I have a dozen ways of making you come around, and I'll use them all if I have to."

"Such as?"

Cowley said with deadly softness, "Did you ever see a piece of fine horseflesh ridden until it died of a burst heart? Even a horse as strong as the gold?"

Fancher stared at him, unbelieving. Cowley went on, in the same soft voice, "Did you ever stop to figure out how many accidents happen to people who work on the range— like Carla does? Do you know how many ways a fire can start in a barn filled with hay, in a stable full of horses or a house full of people?"

Fancher lost his carefully guarded calmness. He rushed at Cowley, his hands clawing. "I'll kill you!" he shouted.

Cowley stepped aside, caught Fancher by the shirtfront and contemptuously lifted him off his feet. "No, you'll marry Carla Sunday." He set Fancher down and turned away.

Lying in his bunk in Ira Moss' small ranch house, Kirk could hear the old man tossing and turning. He said softly, "Better get some sleep, Ira. You're riding out early for Riverport."

"And leaving you alone for at least two nights," Ira said.

"I've lived alone before," Kirk said dryly.

"But not with Weeb after your hide." The old man was worried. "And not with Cowley after Mindy, too. I didn't say much back there in town today, but I know Cowley. The first chance he gets, he'll go after her. She made a laughing stock of him—and that ain't anything he can stand easy."

"Just what did she do?" Kirk asked. He realized how little

he really knew about Mindy. From casual conversation he had learned that she had come to the valley four years ago after selling a profitable restaurant in Portland. Seeking a drier climate, she had chosen Snowy as a growing place without a decent spot for a man and his family to eat and be entertained. Although she was younger than Kirk by more than a year, she was already knowing about the restaurant business, and within a short time she had established herself solidly in Snowy. Beyond that and beyond admiring her not only as a woman but also as a person, he knew little about her.

Ira said, "She riled Cowley about as bad as anyone—unless it's you—ever did. Not long after she was settled in, Cowley tried to get her to knuckle to him the way most of the businessmen do. She made it pretty plain that she was her own woman. Well, the next thing folks began staying away instead of coming the way they had been for dinner and, lots of times, for supper.

"Mindy stood it a while and then she had a card printed up and mailed one to every townsman and rancher who'd been a customer of hers." Ira chuckled in remembrance. "That card said, 'If you're more afraid of threats than you are of food poisoning or indigestion, then stay away from Mindy's Palace. But if you have consideration for your stomach and your reputation as a man, I'm open for business as usual.' And they came back—laughing," Ira went on. "Well, Cowley stomped in and threatened her with a lawsuit for slander. Mindy just looked at him with those gold-flecked eyes of hers wide as a girl's and said, 'Why, Mr. Cowley, I don't recall using your name in my advertisement. Do you really want to get the local businessmen before Judge Breen and have them testify under oath?'

"Cowley up and stomped out. A little while later, Weeb and some of his crew come in and tried to wreck the place. Mindy and her bartender ran them off and she told him never to come back. He did a few nights later and she sent him skyhooting down the street." Ira broke off, laughing until he threatened to choke. "Mindy can shoot the eyes out of a buzzard at a hundred feet in the dead of a dark night, and she knocked the heels off Weeb's boots when he was running. He ain't forgot that and neither has Cowley."

"But Cowley came back," Kirk said.

"Some time later," Ira agreed. "He never says much to Mindy, you'll notice. He only comes because he knows he can be seen there with Judge Breen and Lawyer Parker and other respectable people."

Kirk swallowed a yawn. "Ira, you've just given me one more good reason for settling in Snowy Valley. Not every town has people as fine as Mindy. I think Snowy should keep her."

Before Ira could answer, the sound of a horse hammering toward them through the night brought both men out of their bunks. Kirk reached for his jeans, slid into them and rammed his feet into his waiting boots. Lifting his gun and belt from the nail by the head of his bunk, he strapped them on and moved quickly into the front room. Ira came at his heels, clutching an old Sharps rifle.

Kirk knelt by the front window and carefully drew aside the curtain. The moon was less than half full but there was light enough for him to see the lone rider pounding through the clearing in front of the small house. He unlimbered his gun and then let it fall back.

"It's Arthur on his gold," he told Ira.

Fancher swung the big horse around to the rear and out of their sight. By the time he reached the kitchen door, Kirk was there with a lantern. "Put the horse in the barn," he suggested.

Fancher was pale but there was no sign of fear on his face. It was stiff with anger. "I haven't got time," he said.

"Lex and Weeb are after me. They aren't too far behind."

"How many men does Weeb have along?"

"I counted six when I looked back once; there might be more," Fancher said.

Kirk turned to Ira. "I'll put the horse away while you start the coffee pot." He broke in on Fancher's protest. "If you came here looking for help, that's what you'll get. Running some more won't do you any good. They'll just keep after you. You have to make a stand somewhere."

"I don't have to drag you into it," Fancher said. "I just stopped to borrow some food for the trail."

"Then start with Ira's coffee. It's thick enough to chew," Kirk said. He went out and led the horse to the barn. He found that Fancher had, in addition to his saddle bags, a small gladstone and a large, leather portfolio of his paintings with his easel and paint kit strapped to it. Kirk left the horse saddled but brought the bag and the portfolio inside, stopping long enough to saddle up his roan.

When he got back to the kitchen, he found Fancher sipping Ira's ripe coffee. "What happened?" Kirk asked.

Fancher told him of his discussion with Cowley. "I got too mad to think clearly and I told Lex that not only was I leaving, I was going to write a letter to Carla and tell her everything I'd heard and seen over the years—and that I was sending a copy to Marshal Downes and another to Judge Breen."

"It's a wonder Cowley didn't have you shot right there," Ira observed.

"He probably would have except that he wants me to marry Carla Sunday," Fancher said. "As it was, he locked me in my room and put one of the men on guard. I stopped being mad long enough to do some thinking, and I realized that the only chance I'd have would be to get away as soon as possible. I tricked the guard and hit him on the head, knocking him out." He sounded surprised at his own violence.

"I slipped out with my bag and painting gear and came here. I guess the guard came to and told Lex. They weren't too far behind me."

"Just where did you plan to go to write this letter?" Kirk asked.

"Portland," Fancher said promptly. "The steamer leaves Riverport day after tomorrow. Now if I could get on it, I'd be safe enough—"

"The only road out of the valley is north over the pass," Ira said. "You think Cowley won't block that off?" He glanced at Kirk. "If he can get to Mindy's, he'll be safe enough for a while."

"Not good enough," Kirk said. "He's got to get to Riverport." He smiled suddenly. "Since you're going there tomorrow, old timer, you might as well haul a load in the freight wagon."

"What—Arthur here? What about his horse?"

"Not Arthur, his luggage," Kirk said, pointing to the bag and the portfolio. "That's small enough to hide. And without it, he has a chance of outrunning Cowley tonight—with help." He got up. "I'll pack my saddlebags."

"Wait," Fancher said. "Why should you risk yourself for me this way? You don't owe me anything just because I backed you up at the marshal's today."

"Maybe I'm not risking myself just for you," Kirk said slowly. "Just remember, I know Lex Cowley. When he starts pushing, he never stops until he gets what he wants. Over ten years ago, he wanted my father's ranch to add to his own. My father ended up dead in a stampede during roundup, and I was hauled away from the valley before I could cause too much trouble. Now it's the B-Bar and, it seems, Mindy's cooperation that Cowley wants. I'm tired of letting him have everything his own way. No one has ever pushed back when Cowley started in on them—not for long, anyway. Maybe I just want to see what will happen if someone does."

Ira Moss said, "If you're going, you better hurry. Weeb will turn out as many men as he needs—including Mike Tindall and his miners—if he has to. He can stuff that pass so full of gunhands, not even a jackrabbit could get past."

Kirk left the room. He returned in a few moments, saddlebags over his shoulder and carbine in his hand. "Let's go."

Ira handed Fancher a flour sack of food. "In case you get through the pass, you'll need something to eat before morning," he said.

He closed his mouth, cocking his head. "Riders coming," he said. "Pussyfooting it."

Kirk still his breathing and listened. "So they are." He nodded to Ira. "Put the lamp out and get back into bed. When they come, act like you just woke up. Tell them Fancher isn't here and that I stayed in town all night to get an early start for Riverport in the morning."

"They'll never believe me."

"What difference does that make? It'll give Arthur and me a chance to put some trail under us. And the more distance we can make, the better chance we have of getting out of the valley alive."

V

KIRK and Fancher had their horses in the timber behind the barn when a gunshot cracked on the cool night air. Kirk said briefly, "You stay put. I'm going to watch—in case Ira needs help."

He rode downhill and to the edge of the timber where it met the clearing fronting the house. In the moonlight, he could see Cowley, and four of his crew. Weeb had apparently been doing the shooting, aiming at the sky. He fired again.

"Fancher, come out of there!" he bellowed.

The door opened and Ira Moss stood in his nightshirt, blinking out at them. "What the devil's the idea waking a man up in the middle of the night?"

"I came for Arthur," Cowley said. "And don't tell me he isn't here. I know better."

"If he is, he's not letting me know it," Ira said. "I'm alone far as I know."

"Where's Gannon?" Weeb snapped.

"In town," Ira said, "getting ready for an early start to Riverport come morning." He snorted. "You think you'd be sitting there cocky as a jaybird if Kirk was around?"

Weeb started forward but stopped at a signal from Cowley. "I think the old fool is lying," Weeb grumbled.

"We'll see," Cowley said. "Red, you and One-eye go and check the barn. Weeb, you and Opie get inside and take care of Moss. The rest of you—"

Kirk lifted his carbine from the boot and cocked it. "Nobody's going anywhere right now. That's a pretty piece of moon—all of you reach for it."

Weeb swung in the saddle, bringing down his gun. Kirk whipped a shot by his head. He turned back quickly, holstering his gun and raising his arms. The other riders reached too, including Cowley.

"Now," Kirk said, "Ira, you get your rifle and come back." He raised his voice. "Arthur, you might as well ride here to me. We'll be leaving in a minute."

Cowley said thinly, "This is a fool play, Gannon. You're just asking for trouble for yourself—and for Arthur."

"Fancher's twenty-one and his own man," Kirk said flatly. "Holding him against his will isn't exactly legal. If you want a decision, we can go wake up Judge Breen and ask him."

Ira had shut the door. Now he opened it again and appeared with his Sharps in his hand. He leaned against the jamb, the rifle held casually at his hip. Kirk put his carbine away. None of Cowley's men moved; they all knew how Ira Moss could handle that gun.

Arthur Fancher rode alongside Kirk. Cowley turned his head and stared at them both. "You'd better come home, Arthur. You're not fool enough to think I can let you live to write that letter, but if you come where I can keep an eye on you—and if you marry Carla on Sunday—then there'll be no more trouble."

"You're pretty sure of yourself, Lex, threatening murder with witnesses present."

"If Gannon and Moss don't stop making fools of themselves about this, there won't be any witnesses."

"That's a fair enough warning," Kirk said. "Now let me give one, Cowley. Arthur and I'll be in town long before you can catch up to us. Ira'll see to that. We'll be there with time enough to stop and have a talk with the marshal. If anything happens to Ira Moss, he'll know just where to go and what to do. And don't think he wouldn't like the chance to get you before Judge Breen."

"You might get to town," Crowley said with stifled anger, "but you won't get much farther." He leaned forward, dropping his hands to cup them over his saddle horn.

"And if you should get out of the valley, Arthur will never live to board that steamer. The choice is yours, Gannon. You talked him into acting this way. For his own sake—and yours—you'd be smart to talk some sense into him."

"The decision is Arthur's, not mine," Kirk said.

Fancher spoke to Kirk, ignoring Cowley, "The gold is getting restless. I think he needs a good, hard ride."

Kirk swung the roan. Together they worked to the hill trail and put their horses onto it. Fancher said, "How much chance do they have of catching us?"

"Maybe better than we think. You said you saw a half

dozen of Weeb's men, but he only had four at the house. That means at least two were laying back. They could be riding the valley road, working to cut us off. Or they could be slipping up behind the house to come onto Ira from the back."

"If Lex has him hurt . . ."

"He won't," Kirk said. "Not yet, anyway. Cowley never does any more than he has to. That's one of the secrets of his success. As long as he can hold his patience, Ira's safe enough. It's when that patience slips that trouble will start." He paused and added, "That's what Downes is afraid of—Cowley will forget to keep himself under a tight rein. When he does that, there'll be war in Snowy Valley."

He stopped talking and concentrated on the trail as it began to kink back and forth. Twice he stopped to rest the horses and listen for possible pursuit behind them. He heard nothing. A third time, he drew up on a ridge that gave a view of the valley. If riders were down there, they were too hard to see in the moonlight. The wide road seemed empty.

"We'll go on past town and then cut down on the first trail," Kirk said. "That's when the spark could hit the powder."

They passed well above town and kept the horses moving north. Finally Kirk reined off to his right, following a steep trail toward the valley floor. He moved slowly now, stopping whenever he had a view ahead and peering at each distant shadow, each bit of movement in the moonlight. Halfway to the wagon road leading from Snowy north over the pass and on to Riverport on the Columbia, a stand of tall cottonwoods began. They ran downhill, broke at the road, and then continued on to the willow-lined banks of Snowy Creek. Kirk pulled into the shadow of the trees. Fancher joined him.

"If anyone's after us, they haven't showed themselves yet," he said.

"How could there be?" Fancher wondered aloud. "We'd have heard or seen riders."

"Not if they made a wide sweep east and then cut back toward the foot of the pass," Kirk said. He shrugged. "We can't sit and wait for them to show up, so let's move along. Keep to the shadows and stop at the edge of the road."

They moved on, picking their way through the deep shadows. The slope began to flatten and finally lost itself in the valley. The road slashed across at this point and Kirk pulled up, craning forward to again check the shadows ahead.

"Over to the other side," he snapped, and heeled the roan into a leaping run that took it across the moonlit wagon road and back into shadow. Fancher followed on the gold.

Kirk said worriedly, "I don't like it. Cowley wouldn't have been fool enough not to cover the chance of your getting away from him and riding for the pass." He was staring north now, trying to sort natural movement from anything out of place. But the shadows were deceptive, and he almost missed a shadow that kept changing its shape. Blinking, he rested his eyes and then moved them back to the patch of shadow. He grunted as he saw the movement, he leaned back in the saddle.

"At least two of them in that scrub timber halfway up to the pass," he said. "The way they've positioned themselves, we'd make perfect targets before we ever saw them."

Fancher said, "This isn't your affair, Kirk. Ride home and let me handle my own problem."

"Maybe I have business in Riverport," Kirk said dryly.

"But they'll shoot you down as soon as they see—"

"Then we won't let them see us," Kirk said. "Just stay on my heels."

He put his horse on the opposite side of the line of trees

and then followed the shadows until the shallow bank of Snowy Creek stopped him. Fancher reined alongside. They stared down at the water.

"After all the ranchers take out what they need, there isn't much left this far down the valley," Kirk observed. "It doesn't look more than fetlock deep anywhere."

He glanced toward the pass and then along the twisting line of willows that marked the progress of the creek in the same direction. "It's a chance," he said. "Once in the creek, we'll be hidden by the willows. With luck we can get all the way through the north hills with little more than a cold bath."

Without waiting for an answer, he sent his horse carefully into the creek. Fancher followed, and stayed behind Kirk as he led the way slowly downstream. As he thought, the water was shallow. Finally, the twisting bed straightened and ran into a wall of rock that marked the base of the hills enclosing the valley on the north.

"I know it comes out by the road on the other side of the hills," Fancher whispered, "but how does it get through them?"

"It follows a deep cut," Kirk answered. "It's almost stright down from the cliff at the top of the pass. That's where we have to be careful. If Cowley has any men up there, they could hear us splashing through. And the way that moonlight is angling, it'll show us up. They can stand a hundred feet above us and use us for target practice."

He glanced at Fancher. "You willing to risk it? There are some deep potholes in the cut."

"I can swim," Fancher said. "So can the gold."

Nodding, Kirk led the way forward. Before long the willows stopped and the high rock walls of the cut squeezed in on them. At first the walls were spread at the top, but they narrowed until there was only a thin shaft of moonlight coming down. The canyon made a sudden turn and Kirk lifted a hand in warning.

He stepped his horse more carefully, glancing up every few steps toward the rimrock barely visible on his left. Twice the roan went into potholes that sent icy water surging up and over Kirk's boot tops. Once it foundered, making considerable noise as it splashed back to safer footing. Kirk swore softly and glanced again at the rimrock. Nothing moved there, and with a grunt he urged the horse on.

The water grew colder and deeper as a spring bubbled off the canyon wall to add to the flow. Kirk fought down an urge to push his horse, knowing the danger of the rocky, treacherous bottom.

The canyon began to spread again and with startling suddenness it ended. The creek came into the open and began snaking its way almost placidly through a thick stand of ponderosas.

The sound of a hoof on packed dirt came from the left. Kirk stilled his horse and stopped Fancher with a sharp move of his hand. They stood listening, the horses fetlock deep in the cold water.

The hoofbeats came closer. *Three, no, four,* Kirk thought. He heard Weeb's rough voice. "You sure they didn't get by you, Tindall?"

Mike Tindall, who ran the crew of miners in the east hills, said, "How the devil could they? We had the road blocked."

"Are you sure you saw 'em?"

"I told you I wasn't sure," Tindall answered. He sounded tired and irritated. "But Pete here thinks he saw them coming down from the hill road. Then they disappeared in the cottonwoods."

"They sure as the devil didn't backtrack through the valley," Weeb growled, "or me and Opie'd have seen 'em." There was a long silence. Then he said, "By God, I know what happened! Gannon rode the creek. They could be on this side right now." Hoofs scratched at the ground. "Get your guns out. We'll have us a look."

Kirk turned to Fancher. "Move on as quietly as you can. The first chance you get, climb out of the creek. If we get separated, make for that big rock slide about three miles down the trail. We can camp there."

"I know it," Fancher said. He put the gold around Kirk and moved on and out of sight. Kirk remained where he was for a few moments, his head cocked. Fancher rode his horse with surprising quiet. Kirk doubted if Weeb and his men, blundering through brush now, could hear anything but their own movements.

Quickly he sent his horse forward, up the bank and onto dry land. He trotted it down to a thick stand of timber. Easing out of the saddle, he took his carbine and moved to where he could get a view of the road and the thin timber he had just come through.

He saw the dark bulk of Weeb outlined on the night. He was coming from the direction of the creek. Then he saw a smaller form on the road. He thought it was Opie. Opie stood in the saddle, pointing.

"There goes the gold!" he shouted. "I just saw him."

Kirk swore at Fancher's carelessness. Weeb bellowed back to Opie, "Keep him in sight." He turned and crashed his way back to the road, two riders following him.

Kirk stood and watched them coming openly, guns drawn. They were obviously contemptuous of Arthur Fancher, even if he should be armed. Weeb cried, "There. Straight ahead." His rifle lifted and he fired.

Kirk swore again. He could see nothing down the road. But he could hear the cry of a man and the wild thrashing of a horse as it smashed into the trees lining the road.

VI

KIRK LET THE four men ride past. Then he stepped into the open, lifted his carbine and snapped off two quick shots. Weeb's hat jerked free of his head. Mike Tindall ducked as lead whined past his ear.

"That's far enough!" Kirk snapped.

Four horses reined up sharply. "Gannon, by God!" Weeb cried.

"Drop your guns," Kirk said levely.

Weeb's voice was thick with satisfaction. "You're too late, Gannon. I already dropped Fancher. Nothing you can do's going to chance that."

Kirk had no answer for that, but Arthur Fancher did. His voice came strong and clear from a short distance ahead. "You ran me into the trees, Weeb. I'm standing behind one now—with a rifle steadied on a branch. And it's aimed at you."

"Boxed!" Opie said shrilly. "They boxed us, Weeb."

"The devil they have!" Weeb cried. He slammed rowels into his horse's flanks, sending it spurting up the trail. Tindall and the others followed close on Weeb's heels. Kirk ducked back into the timber, stepped out as they passed, and hurried them on their way with two more shots. He stood in the roadway, watching as they pushed their horses up a rise and out of sight.

Getting the roan, he rode down to where Fancher waited. "That was a nice trick," Kirk said.

"If it worked," Fancher answered. "Weeb doesn't give up easily."

"By the time they stop running, their horses won't be in any shape to ride back this way—not tonight," Kirk assured him. He chucked suddenly. "I'd like to see that gun you had braced in a tree crotch."

Fancher held up a length of dried branch about the thickness of a rifle muzzle at one end. Laughing, he tossed it away and turned the gold down the trail. "You plan to make Riverport tonight?"

"No problem," Kirk assured him. "And the hotel's better sleeping than the ground."

They rode on, stopping to rest the horses at the rock slide Kirk had mentioned earlier. He built a fire and made coffee from the gear in his saddlebags.

"Weeb might not come after us tonight," Fancher said, "but he will tomorrow."

"I expect him to," Kirk agreed. "I look for Cowley as well." He blew on his coffee. "What are your plans after you leave the boat?"

Fancher huddled up to the fire. "I'll got to Portland and try to support myself with my art," he said. He added dryly, "Maybe I can get work painting signs."

"Just how much money do you have?" Kirk asked quietly.

Fancher took the question as meant, not as prying. "Enough to get me to Portland and keep me a few weeks." He hesitated and said, "I don't have enough to ship the gold here, though. For a while I thought about trying to sell him in Riverport, but I hate the thought someone who didn't appreciate him might become his owner."

"You have a lot of yourself in that horse," Kirk said.

"My mother gave him to me not long before she died. He was just a colt then. I've always been a good rider—but no other horse ever felt like this one under me. I guess you could see he means a whole lot."

"Then don't sell him," Kirk said. "Send him back with me. I'll keep him for you until you can send for him—or better yet, let Carla keep him and exercise him for you."

Fancher stared at him. "Carla! Don't you realize what she's going to think of me when she finds out I've run away? As if I'm scared to marry her!"

"Maybe at first," Kirk said. "But once she hears the truth —and especially after she gets your letter, then she'll think differently."

Fancher ran a hand over his lean features. "I hope so," he whispered miserably. "I hope she'll understand." He took a deep breath. "I won't ask her to keep the gold for me, but I'll give him to her. She thinks a lot of him. Maybe she'll take him—if you or Ira explain what happened."

"We'll do our best," Kirk said.

Finishing his coffee, he cleaned up, doused the fire, and then they rode on. It was growing cold and was after midnight when they rode down the slope to Riverport, stretching up from the Columbia along one steep street. A sleepy desk clerk in the hotel gave them a room with two beds and the night boy at the livery let them stall their horses. They spent a little time rubbing the animals down and seeing that they had a good feed of oats. Then they went back to the hotel and managed to get undressed and into bed before they fell asleep.

The next day passed more quietly than Kirk expected. With Kirk along as bodyguard, Fancher spent his morning buying things he needed for the trip. In the middle of the afternoon, the steamer chugged in from its last stop, Wallula-Under-the-Hill on the Washington side of the water. Fancher arranged for his passage. By then it was supper time.

With the evening light fading, they sat in the hotel room, Fancher sorting out his paintings and drawings and Kirk watching. Finally Fancher held up a small canvas. It was a fine painting of the gold rearing up to paw at the sky, wind riffling his mane.

"I'd like you to have this if you want," he said.

Before Kirk could answer, footsteps sounded outside. Kirk

48

came to his feet, his hand dropping to the .44 on his hip. A sharp knock on the panel demanded entry.

A voice said with brusque impatience, "Arthur, this is Lex. Open up and let me in!"

Kirk glanced at Fancher. He stood by the painting-littered bed, his face drained of color. Outside, Cowley snapped, "Arthur, I told you to open this door!"

Fancher took a deep breath. "God has spoken," he whispered thinly. He nodded. "Let him in. I faced him once. I can do it again."

Kirk unlocked and opened the door, stepping back as he did. His hand was still on his gun butt.

Cowley came inside, moving with his customary arrogance —with the sureness of a man convinced that his money and his power gave him control over any situation.

His eyes raked Kirk coldly. "I've told you before about interfering in my affairs, Gannon. You've done it for the last time." He dismissed Kirk contemptuously and turned to Fancher. "I came to take you home."

"We've been over that already," Fancher said in a controlled voice.

"Get packed up. I talked to Carla. She asked me to tell you to come back."

"Did you explain to her why you're so eager to see us married?" Fancher demanded. "Did you tell her what will happen if we don't marry—happen to her?"

Cowley's jawline jumped as his impatience fought with his self control. "How much of that nonsense have you told Gannon?"

"I've told nobody anything but the truth. I told them what you said to me yesterday. And I intend to put nothing but the truth in my letter."

Cowley said softly, "Then you haven't written your lies yet?"

Kirk said softly, "Don't let that give you ideas, Cowley.

49

The next time any of your bully boys come after Arthur, I'll do more than shoot off a hat."

Cowley ignored him. Fancher said, "Now get out and leave us alone, Lex. I'm taking the morning steamer and I want to get some sleep."

Cowley addressed Kirk now. "You should take the same boat, Gannon. There's no place in Snowy Valley for you."

"I'm making a place for myself," Kirk answered. "When I've finished the dam, I'm buying a piece of property." He opened the door and stood aside.

Cowley stared from one man to the other, his nostrils flaring. Then he strode into the hall, turned and marched down it, not looking back. Kirk waited until he disappeared. Then he closed and locked the door.

Fancher sat down, trembling. Kirk shook his head at him. "Don't let any man ever tell you again that you lack the belly for anything. Not after what you just did."

Fancher shrugged it away. "I'm worried about what he'll try to do to you. Lex doesn't make idle threats."

"I can handle myself," Kirk said shortly. He picked up the painting Fancher had offered him. "I'll be glad to take this. But it might make things a little easier for me if you wrote the instructions about my giving the gold to Carla on the back—as a kind of receipt for my having the horse with me."

Fancher nodded. Taking his paints and a brush, he wrote quickly on the clean side of the canvas, "This is to certify that Kirk Gannon is delivering my gold horse to Carla Belden—to whom I give it as a gift." He dated the message and signed it with his fancy signature. He laid the painting on the dresser.

"It'll be dry enough to roll up by morning," he said.

Stripping to his longjohns, he started to climb into bed. He stared at the litter of paintings, spent a few moments putting them in the portfolio and then crawled under the blankets. Kirk followed, blowing out the lamp.

Fancher said out of the darkness, "I still don't see why you should risk yourself for me this way."

"Maybe it isn't all for you," Kirk said. "Now get to sleep. That boat leaves early."

Kirk had almost drifted into sleep when he heard a soft footfall and a tap at the door. Frowning, he came to his feet, reaching for his gun under his pillow. He padded to the door and drew it carefully open. He slammed it quickly.

"Light the lamp," he said thickly. "And get your jeans on."

Fancher came blearily awake. "Who is it?"

"A lady," Kirk said. When the lamp flared up, he reached for his jeans and shirt. After Fancher was dressed, Kirk opened the door. Mindy and Ira Moss walked in.

Mindy wore a split leather skirt, a flannel shirt and vest, and had her hair knotted at the nape of her neck so that the broad-brimmed hat she wore fit on her finely shaped head. She grinned impishly at Kirk.

"That was a scurvy trick, wasn't it?"

Kirk grinned back. "What are you doing here? Don't you trust Ira to buy your supplies for you?"

"I trust Ira. I don't trust Lex Cowley." Mindy took the chair. Ira perched on the edge of Kirk's bed. Ira said, "We got here some time back, but we been a little busy. That's why we didn't come see you sooner." He nodded at the door. "Cowley and Weeb and Opie passed us on the road today. They thought about stopping for a mite of a visit, but Mindy sitting on the box with her rifle in her lap maybe discouraged them. So they only stopped long enough for Cowley to say, 'You seem to have the idea that Snowy can't get along without you and your place of business,' to Mindy. And he rode on.

"We didn't see him again until he come stomping down

the stairs and out through the lobby. That was when we was coming into the hotel. We figured from the look on his face he hadn't got very far with Arthur here. We figured, too, that he wasn't through trying. So we kind of waited in our rooms, and sure enough not too long ago Weeb and Opie come sneaking up the hall."

Ira paused to chuckle. "You should have seen their faces when Mindy opened her door on one side of the hall and I opened mine on the other, and we stood there with our guns looking at them. They hotfooted it, I can tell you."

"Our thanks," Kirk said, as Fancher whooped with laughter like a delighted small boy. "You had no trouble with them last night at the Oval-M, Ira?"

"None," Ira said. "They got tired looking at my gun and rode off." He coughed and looked away from Fancher. "I had me a ride too. I went to Carla's after Cowley left."

Fancher looked unhappy. Ira said, "I've knowed her since the days when Sam Belden and I was partners and she was a little tyke coming to visit. She kind of treats me like an uncle." He grimaced. "But she didn't act much like she believed me when I laid everything out for her—Fancher's leaving and why and all."

"She can't believe anyone could be like Lex really is," Fancher said.

"I kept after her," Ira said, "until she agreed to ride in town with me and stay at Mindy's. I told her to keep an eye out and if she saw Cowley with Weeb and some others of the L-in-C crew hotfooting it north, she'd know they were coming here after Arthur. Then she'd know I was telling the truth."

"I talked with her last night until late," Mindy said. "She understands, but she isn't very happy about it. No woman could be with her marriage date so close."

"I suppose she expected me to stand up and fight Lex," Fancher said in a misery-ridden voice.

"I'm afraid so," Mindy answered. "She said that's what she would do if she learned Ira told the truth."

Fancher said, "Thanks for trying for me. Maybe later it'll be easier for her."

"It'll take a long time," Mindy said. "She's pretty deeply in love." She got up. "I think you can both sleep now. But be careful in the morning, Kirk. Cowley hasn't given up."

Kirk walked a short way down the hall with Mindy and Ira. He said, "Don't look for me until about evening day after tomorrow. I'm going to ride with Arthur down to the next port. And I'll be going a little slower from here home." He explained about his taking the gold back with him.

Ira nodded. "When you get on that boat in the morning, Mindy and me'll be down to the docks, loading supplies."

Kirk understood his meaning and thanked them with a nod. Returning to the room, he found Fancher in bed and apparently asleep. Quietly he undressed and climbed into his own bed. This time, he hoped, he would make it through until morning.

With the first daylight, he and Fancher went down to the dock where the small river steamer huffed and puffed at its moorage. Fancher was walking, having left the gold in the livery stable. Kirk rode the roan, and when they reached a warehouse a block from the gangplank, he reined in and motioned Fancher to stop.

"You stay here until you see me at that boat," he said.

He rode around the warehouse, reaching the dock at its far end. The steamer had unloaded last evening and bales and boxes of goods were stacked all around—making, Kirk thought, fine places for snipers to hide and watch the gangplank. Leaving the horse, he went forward on foot. He moved softly, checking each pile of goods before moving on.

From the open door of a warehouse, Ira hailed him in a low tone. He said, "Cowley rode for home a while ago—alone."

"What about Weeb and Opie?" Kirk asked.

Ira nodded toward the river, gray in the early morning light. "Their horses are over that way, behind them bales. But they ain't there," he added pointedly.

Looking closer at the freight piled up to be loaded on the wagon drawn up by the warehouse, Kirk saw Ira's Sharps rifle. He looked farther but found no sign of Mindy.

"You were waiting for me?"

Ira nodded. Kirk said, "Where's Mindy. Did she . . ."

Ira said, "She couldn't wait. She wasn't as sure as me you was coming around this way before you took Fancher to the boat. So she went Weeb hunting."

Kirk swore softly. "She's in enough trouble with Cowley already!" he said angrily. "If she keeps it up, he'll do more than run her out of the valley. He'll have her killed."

VII

IRA PICKED up his rifle. "Mindy can take care of herself," he said. But he was talking to empty air.

Kirk was already back onto the dock, threading his way between bales and piles of merchandise. He saw something move ahead of him on the right and dropped his hand to his gun. Then he saw that it was Mindy.

She had a carbine in her hands and she was moving softly around the end of a stack of boxes. Kirk moved quickly after her, going around the other side of the boxes to intercept her. He stopped short.

Ahead of him was Weeb, his belly down on a bale, his feet sticking past the end and his eye squinted at the sights of a rifle. A few feet away, Opie lay in a smiliar position. Both men had their guns aimed through slits between two bales. Kirk was sure they were aimed at the gangplank leading from the dock to the deck of the little steamer.

Kirk drew his gun. He saw Mindy glance at him and nod as she raised her rifle, aiming it at Weeb. Kirk said softly, "Let the gun lie there and get on your feet, Opie."

Weeb moved first, pulling his gun back, turning, and rolling to his feet in a motion surprisingly fast for a man of his bulk. He stopped when Mindy's voice said coolly, "That's far enough."

Weeb swore. His head swung from Mindy to Kirk. He said in a thick voice, "Boxed again, by God! And by a woman . . ."

Kirk motioned with his gun. "I said to move, Opie. And leave your gun. You too, Weeb. Now!"

"I ain't riding without my guns," Opie said shrilly. "There's road agents in these parts."

"None that aren't friends of yours," Kirk answered dryly. "And you'll ride or I'm going to start shooting. I'll worry about the local law later."

He moved his gun again. Reluctantly Opie crawled to his feet, leaving his rifle. Weeb studied Kirk and then laid his gun on the bale behind him. Kirk said, "Put your handguns with them, gents."

They did as he ordered. Weeb said hoarsely, "This is the last time, Gannon. If I ever see you again, you ain't going to live to tell about it."

"I'll be in town to keep my date for that fight you agreed to," Kirk said pleasantly. He herded them ahead of him, Mindy at his side. When they reached their horses, he ordered, "Now walk them until I tell you to climb aboard."

Ira Moss came from behind a stack of boxes, with his rifle in hand. "Just in case you missed 'em," he explained and grinned at Kirk.

Kirk glanced at Mindy. "That was a crazy stunt you pulled, going after them alone."

She stepped alongside Ira. "I agree," she said with a smile. "Sometimes I act almost as loco as you."

Kirk motioned for Weeb and Opie to start walking. When he reached his own horse, he climbed aboard. Mindy and Ira were still close behind. He called, "I can handle it from here. If these two or any other of Cowley's men give you trouble on the way home, remember that the marshal knows all about it. And I'm telling the sheriff here."

The story about Marshal Downes knowing was a bit stretched, but both Mindy and Ira nodded as if they knew all about it. Weeb stared up at Kirk. "Nobody'll do nothing to them, Gannon—because they're getting a week to pack up, sell out, and leave Snowy Valley. But the same don't go for you. Just you don't come back at all."

"Get on your horses and ride," Kirk snapped. He followed them a short distance and then turned back to tell Fancher to get aboard the boat. The first whistle had already blown.

Fancher showed his surprise when Kirk stepped out of the saddle and led the roan up the gangplank. "You've done enough for me," he said. His face turned pink above his beard. "I don't need a bodyguard the rest of my life, Kirk."

"I'm just riding to the next port," Kirk assured him. "Cowley isn't a man to give up easily," he said. "Nor one to overlook any chance." He nodded at the horse already in the pens built on the afterdeck. "That's a livery stable horse," he said. "It was in the stall next to your horse last night. Now, who would rent a horse just for the pleasure of giving it a boatride—and sending it back to Riverport the same way?"

"You think Lex has a man on board?"

"He wouldn't have had if Weeb and Opie had been successful," Kirk said. He told Fancher what had happened on the dock.

Fancher started forward. "I'm going to my cabin to write those letters—right now," he said.

Kirk followed him, stopping only long enough to pay the purser for his passage and that of the roan. He sat in the small cabin, watching as Fancher quickly wrote his first letter. He put it in an envelope and addressed it to Marshal Downes. He took more time over his second letter, now and then crossing out a word or an entire sentence. Finally he took a fresh sheet of paper and copied his original letter. He addressed this to Carla Belden and then gave both letters to Kirk.

"Could you mail these at the next port?"

Looking briefly at the envelopes, Kirk handed them back. "Mail them from Portland," he said curtly. "That'll be time enough."

Fancher stared at him, frowning. Then he took the letters and put them in his portfolio. Kirk knew he had hurt the boy, that he didn't understand why Kirk had acted that way. But maybe he would understand later, Kirk hoped. Maybe, when he got ready to mail those letters, he would realize how final an action that would be—how completely it cut him off from returning to Carla.

Kirk said, "Let's take a look around. Cowley owns people in the valley I haven't met yet. Maybe you can spot the right one."

They made a tour of the deck. The boat was moving well with the downsteam current. It wouldn't be long before they docked at the next port. If he didn't find Cowley's man by then, Kirk knew he would have to go on. Already he could feel the pressure of time; he wanted to get this finished and start back for Snowy Valley.

Finishing the round of the boat, Fancher opened the door to his cabin. "Nobody I ever saw before is aboard," he said. "I—"

Kirk knocked Fancher's hand from the door latch with one quick move and shouldered Fancher aside, sending him staggering down the corridor. At the same time he threw himself flat, rolling after Fancher.

A gunshot boomed in the narrow space. A bullet splintered the door panel and smashed against the bulkhead opposite. Kirk came to his knees, his gun drawn. The door had swung shut. Now he reached out a cautious hand and lifted the latch. Again he got down, but in front of the door now. Reaching out a second time, he pushed the door wide. His gun was up, aimed at the man standing in the middle of the small cabin.

"All right, Tindall, drop your hardware," Kirk said softly.

Mike Tindall was a big man in rough, miner's clothing. He held his gun as most men more accustomed to holding a pick and shovel would. He stared at the muzzle of Kirk's .44 and then let his own gun drop to the floor.

Kirk got to his feet, picked up the gun, and motioned to Fancher. Footsteps could be heard coming quickly toward them. "How do you want me to tell it, Tindall—that the gun went off by accident or that you were trying to kill Arthur?"

"I wasn't trying to kill nobody," Tindall said. "I seen his name on the passenger list and I figured I'd drop in and have a cup of coffee with him since we're both from the same place. I . . ."

Kirk stared at the deep-set eyes almost hidden by Tindall's bushy, dark beard. He said, "Do you want to tell it that way before a court of law?"

Tindall stared at him. "What the devil do you want me to say, Gannon?"

"Say that it was an accident and that you're getting off with me at the next port—and pay for the damage."

Tindall scowled. "Maybe I ain't ready to get off."

The purser and a deck officer arrived. Kirk said quickly, "My friend here was showing me his gun and it went off.

58

Sorry about it. He'll pay for the damage if you'll figure it up."

Tindall opened his mouth and shut it again. Kirk said, "Can you do that right now? We're both getting off as soon as you dock."

"We're already docked and unloading," the deck officer said.

Kirk realized now that the deck was a good deal steadier under his feet. He grinned. "I guess in the excitement we didn't notice. How much is the damage?"

The purser made a quick calculation. Grudgingly, Tindall paid in gold. Then he followed Kirk on deck and back to the horses. He saddled and mounted the rented animal. Kirk dressed the roan and got on. Fancher accompanied him to the head of the gangplank.

Bending down, Kirk thrust out a hand. "Maybe I'll see you again, Arthur. If not, good luck with your painting."

Fancher said abruptly, "Thanks for everything, Kirk," turned, and hurried away.

Kirk followed Tindall off the boat and through the small town. Once beyond it, they hit the Oregon Trail and turned east.

Tindall rode in sulky silence. It was mid-morning now and the sun was warm in a cloudless sky. Around noon, Kirk pulled off the trail. "Let's make some coffee."

"I didn't bring nothing with me."

"I'll let you have some of mine," Kirk said pleasantly. Dismounting, he ordered Tindall to build a small fire, draw water at a spring near by, and make the coffee. When it was done, Kirk brought some bread and cold beef from his saddlebags and gave half to Tindall. Tindall ate, still silent. Finished, Kirk had him clean the small camp and douse the fire. Then, the gear stowed back to his saddlebags, he mounted his horse, caught up the reins of the other horse and started off.

"You can't leave a man stranded like this!" Tindall cried. "There's a settlement a good walk ahead," Kirk said. "Move fast enough and you can make it before dark. I'll see that the horse gets back to the livery where you rented it. I'll leave your gun there, too. You can get it back when you pay the bill."

Tindall cursed until he was hoarse. Kirk rode off, leading the other animal. Some distance along, he changed to the other horse to give his a rest.

It was darkening when he rode into Riverport. He turned both horses in at the livery, explaining that Tindall would be along the next day, and giving the liveryman the .44 to hold until Tindall came. Then with his saddlebags over his shoulder, Kirk went to the hotel and took a room.

He spent part of the morning at the hardware store checking on some equipment he was thinking of buying once he got settled in Snowy Valley. The hardware man said, "I can order it out of Portland any time you want."

"I'll be back in two weeks or so if I can use it," Kirk said. "If you don't see me by then, figure it's no sale." Nodding pleasantly, he left.

Two weeks, he thought as he walked to the livery. *By then, I'll either have a piece of Snowy Valley to call my own or I'll be planted under it.* One way or another, he knew, things had to come to a head soon. Cowley had been pushed as far as he could stand. It wasn't going to take much more to make him lose that carefully guarded patience and use his force openly.

Kirk mulled over it as he rode up the trail for Snowy. Most of the time he led the gold but now and then he rested the roan by transferring his saddle. He could understand why Fancher thought so much of the big, pale horse. It was magnificently gaited and spirited without being unruly. He could feel the difference when he got back on his own mount.

He rode more carefully once he left the wide Oregon Trail for the narrower wagon road sloping upward to Snowy Valley. As the timber thickened, he checked for a possible ambush before moving along. But he saw no one by the time he reached the foot of the pass. The sun had set and dusk was moving in. He came to the flat top of the pass with only the last, lingering fingers of daylight to show him the way.

At the far end, near the drop to the valley, sat an abandoned stage rest-stop, wind and weather scoured. Kirk was opposite it when he saw movement from the corner of his eye. He dropped a hand to his gun and then let his fingers fall away. Men were closing in on him, two coming from behind the building and two from behind a gallows tree on the flat to the west. Kirk recognized Weeb and Opie and, when the other two men came close enough, he saw that Red and One-eye Jones had joined the party.

"Well, well," Weeb said. "Look what Gannon's towing—Fancher's horse. I'd say we caught us a horse thief!"

He rode close to Kirk, grinning. "You know what happens to horse thieves in these parts, Gannon. We string 'em up. All right, boys, unwind the rope!"

VIII

KIRK realized Weeb wasn't playing a joke. He meant to do what he threatened—hang Kirk as a horse thief.

"If you've got a complaint," Kirk said levelly, "let's take it to the law." His eyes kept moving from man to man, looking for a mistake, for a chance to go for his gun.

"Hell," Weeb said. His teeth showed briefly in a wide grin. "I ain't going to bother a busy marshal with a little thing like this. All right, Red, rig up the rope." He waggled his gun at Kirk. "You just keep them hands high."

"I'm delivering this horse for Fancher," Kirk said quietly. "I can prove that. You string me up, Weeb, and Downes will have the excuse he needs to charge you with murder."

"Ain't that nice of you, helping Fancher out that way," Opie said in his shrill voice.

Kirk could hear Red over by the gallows tree and he cursed himself for having assumed all the danger was back on the trail. He had let up his guard before he should have. Now he merely stared stonily at Opie.

Red came up behind Kirk, cut the gold's lead rein and sent the horse trotting off. Then he slapped the roan on the rump, sending it toward the old tree.

"Drop your hands easy," Red said.

Kirk let his hands come down, pulling them around toward his back. He bent forward suddenly, slashing his heels into the roan's flanks. It leaped forward. Kirk caught the reins and jerked the roan in a see-saw run across the flat. He drew his .44, turned, and snapped a shot at Red. His bullet tore the gun from Red's hand, making him scream with pain.

Opie fired at Kirk and missed. Weeb aimed carefully and sent a shot that whined off rock by the roan's front hoofs. It twisted in sudden fright, rearing. Kirk felt himself leaving the saddle and he grabbed for leather. The horse came down with a solid thud. Kirk slid to one side and then righted himself. He lifted his head and saw Weeb directly in front of him, gun leveled at his chest.

"Throw down that gun," Weeb snapped. "And you come down with it."

Kirk measured his chance against Weeb's staring gun, shrugged, and tossed his own to the dirt. Then he dismounted slowly. As long as he remained alive he had a chance, he figured.

Weeb said, "Tie him up."

Red, still shaking his gun hand, came forward with One-eye at his side. Suddenly Red stepped forward and slammed his left fist into Kirk's kidney. Kirk twisted and went forward with pain. One-eye slammed him on the temple, driving him to his knees. Red's big boot lashed out, catching him in the ribs. He went down. Red kicked him again, this time in the stomach. Kirk rolled over, retching.

Red and One-eye hauled him to his feet. Red hit him twice more in the body, not marking his face on Weeb's snapped instructions. Then Weeb said, "That's enough fun, boys; we ain't got all night."

Kirk staggered as if he might fall and then made a dive for his gun still lying in the dirt. His fingers closed over the butt just as Red's boot hit his head. He rolled away, fighting the blackness that threatened to drown him.

He was barely aware of his hands being tied behind his back, of his body being lifted into the saddle, and his feet put into the stirrups while he was led to the tree. Then his feet were pushed free and the roughness of a noose settled around his neck. He could feel, but he could see nothing through the mist filling his eyes.

Weeb's voice came out of the blackness, "All right, make sure the end of that rope's good and tight around the trunk."

"It's tight," Red said thickly.

"Let me kick the horse out from under him," Opie pleaded.

"That's my pleasure," Weeb said softly. "All mine."

Kirk heard Weeb's horse moving forward and around the roan. "All right," Weeb said gloatingly, "here's one horse thief that won't work in Snowy Valley." He laughed. His voice broke off to lift in a shout, and Kirk heard the slap of his hat against the roan's rump.

The horse surged forward.

Kirk felt the rope bruise his neck, and for the first time he could accept the idea that he was going to die. His voice choked out a soft word to the roan. It stopped abruptly, leaving the rope stretched from Kirk's neck to the tree. Weeb swore and rode forward. "Move, damn you!"

The roan jumped again. The pressure of the rope caught at Kirk's windpipe. A roaring filled his ears, drowning all other sounds. Then the pressure disappeared. Kirk felt himself lifted, felt himself falling, felt his body slam into the hard ground. The knot under his ear was loosened and the roaring began to ebb from his ears.

Kirk sucked in the cool night air and opened his eyes. He blinked and they cleared. He saw Weeb straightened up after having loosened the rope. Weeb saving him? Kirk wondered if he was still alive—or if death was such a twisted joke.

A commanding voice snapped, "Now cut his hands free. And if your knife touches anything but that rope, you'll be using it to dig lead out of yourself." It was Mindy's voice, Kirk realized.

"We caught Gannon here with Fancher's horse," Weeb protested. "We got a right to hang a horse thief."

"You've got a right to take him to the law," Mindy said. "And that's where we're all going—to see the marshal." A gun cracked. Dirt splattered on Kirk as lead whipped dirt by Weeb's feet. "Now cut him free."

Weeb bent and hurriedly slashed the cord around Kirk's wrists. He moved quickly away. Kirk pulled his arms in front of his body and began massaging blood back into his wrists and hands. Carefully, slowly, he sat up and looked around. The movement made his eyesight blur at first, but finally he was able to pierce the thickening twilight.

Weeb and Opie were on foot, their hands held away from their sides. Red and One-eye were still on horseback but they were too busy reaching for sky to think about going anywhere. Kirk moved his head. To the south, at the top of the trail, Mindy sat her horse. A rifle was held almost casually in her hands.

"You're messing a little too much in my affairs," a ripe voice said from darkness by the abandoned building. Kirk turned to look that way. He was not surprised to see Cowley on his big horse.

Mindy leaned forward and her voice was filled with contempt. "Why don't you come right out and say you're going to try to get even with me for interfering with you, Cowley? Or do you plan to keep on hiding behind words the way you hid behind that building?"

Kirk could see Cowley's gloved hands clench the reins. "I don't hide," he said in a tight voice. "Now drop that rifle. I can shoot from here with no trouble at all."

Kirk thought it strange that none of Cowley's crew made any move. They kept their positions, hands held high—as if Cowley hadn't been there at all.

Mindy said pleasantly, "Ira, what kind of a target does Cowley make?"

From the tumble of rocks near the edge of the flat, where it dropped down to the river, Ira Moss stood up, Sharps in hand. "He makes a fine, big target," he said slowly. "Just like any big bag of wind would."

Kirk turned to watch Cowley. He could see the man fighting for self-control, almost lose it, and then gain it. Cowley's hand moved in the dimness as he holstered his gun.

"Let them have their fun," Cowley said, "We've got ranch work to do, so let's ride."

"Oh, no," Mindy snapped. "These four are riding to see the marshal. I'm charging them with attempted murder."

Kirk got to his feet and walked slowly to the roan. With an effort he hauled himself aboard. "I'll bring that charge myself," he said. His voice sounded unsteady to his ears.

"You haven't got a leg to stand on," Cowley sneered. "You came here openly with Arthur's horse—as if you owned it. What did you expect?"

"I told Weeb I was delivering him and that I have proof," Kirk said in a steadier tone. "He couldn't be bothered to listen."

"There are five of us that say you're lying," Cowley answered.

"We'll discuss it in the marshal's office," Mindy said. "Opie, get Weeb's gun—and those from Red and One-eye. Heap them under the tree."

"And bring me my guns," Kirk ordered.

Opie remained where he was until Cowley snapped, "Get moving. We can't sit here all night."

Opie did as he was told, picking up all the guns, including Cowley's, and stacking them under the gallows tree. He gingerly brought Kirk his .44 and his carbine and backed away quickly.

Kirk rode to Mindy. "My thanks—for what little words can say."

"It'll even out," she said. Her smile warmed him. "They aren't through with either one of us."

"They never will be until one side is dead or out of Snowy Valley," Kirk answered. "Shall we ride?"

"We'll go ahead. Ira can herd them."

They started down the switchback that dropped from the pass to the valley. It was dark and the lights of Snowy made a blotch of yellow in the distance. Here and there the lights from a ranch pinpricked the night.

"We got back earlier today," Mindy said. "We were wondering when you'd return when it occurred to both of us that you might run into some kind of trouble." She turned her head and smiled at him again. "When it started to darken, I began to fret, and finally Ira told me to leave the Palace to itself and ride with him. Thank heaven I did."

Kirk opened his mouth to agree and then gasped as pain lanced through him. The excitement that had carried him above pain had drained away and he began to feel the effects of the beating he had taken. He rode in silence, one hand clinging to the horn. Every stride of the roan made pain shoot through his back and ribs and head. By the time they clattered across the small bridge and into Snowy, he was fighting the mist rising again into his eyes.

The town was quiet at this hour with all but the saloons, Mindy's, and the jail closed for the night. As they passed her Palace, Cowley rode closer to her.

"You had a good thing going here. It's too bad you weren't smart enough to know how to keep it."

"Save your threats," Mindy said. "Meaner varmints than you have tried to give me trouble."

Cowley shrugged and dropped back. Mindy led the way to the hitching rail in front of the jail and stepped easily from the saddle. When Kirk tried to follow, he felt himself falling. With an effort he turned and caught the rail to steady himself.

Mindy was quickly at his side. Kirk said thickly, "Saddle-bags—canvas," and slumped.

He lost track of time. Vaguely he remembered hearing Mindy's voice snap orders for Weeb and Cowley to support him into the marshal's office. He barely felt the blow Weeb slammed into his sore ribs when they were turned from Mindy's view.

He began to come around slowly. He was in a chair in Downes' office, the lanky, inquiring face of Doc Irmser peering down at him. He could hear voices raised in argument. He felt something rough in his fingers and realized it was the rolled picture of the gold Fancher had given him.

"Gannon needs to get to bed," the doctor said. "His ribs need wrapping up and . . ."

"Soon," Downes said. His voice was tired and irritable. "Can he talk yet?"

"I can talk," Kirk said slowly. The doctor moved away

and he looked around. Weeb and his crew stood lined against one wall. Ira stood holding his Sharps. Mindy and Cowley were both seated, Cowley with a contemptuous look on his face.

"This is a waste of time," he said. "My men did what they thought was right."

Kirk said, "I told Weeb I had proof that I was taking the horse to Carla. He wouldn't listen."

"You didn't say—"

"Stop lying or I'll put a bullet in your gullet!" Ira snapped.

"You'll put that gun away in here!" Downes told him.

"Why, so he can start a fight and kill Kirk?" Ira demanded shrilly. "You know danged well what kind of varmints you're dealing with, Marshal. Stop pussyfooting with them."

"I'm the law," Downes said. "I act like the law, not like a vigilante mob." He waited until Ira set his gun aside. Then he added wearily, "I'll hear your stories—one at a time."

He nodded to Kirk and listened as Kirk spoke slowly, telling his story exactly as he remembered it happening. He finished by saying, "If it hadn't been for Mindy here, I'd be dead now. I still can't figure how she got that rope cut so fast, but—"

"Cut!"

"Cut!" Ira snorted. "She shot it clean through while she was sitting a moving horse—that's how."

Downes waved him to silence. "You claim Fancher gave you the horse to deliver to Carla. Can you prove that, Gannon?"

Kirk lifted the painting and carefully unrolled it. Cowley said in a disgusted voice, "I have two or three paintings of the gold. What does that prove?"

Kirk could feel himself growing dizzy again. He said in a thick voice, "On the back," and thrust the painting toward the marshal. The movement sent his body forward, out of the chair. He tried to recover himself but his dizziness was greater than his will. He felt the blackness closing over him and he could do nothing about it.

When Kirk opened his eyes he found himself in the hard, narrow bed in Doctor Irmser's hospital, the spare room in his rambling house. He had been stripped and Irmser was busily wrapping a cloth tightly around his middle.

"Nothing broken," the doctor said when he saw that Kirk's eyes were open. "But a lot of bruises. You'll be laid up for a few days."

"I can't waste that much time."

Irmser stood back and stared down at him. "Just remember, Gannon, the sooner you're up and around, the sooner someone's going to try to put a bullet in you. And I can't heal that up like I can this." He tapped Kirk's bruised ribs.

"My advice," he went on, "is for you to rest here and when you leave, ride back where you came from—as fast as you can get there."

IX

A LONG night's sleep put Kirk on his feet, and by midafternoon he left the hospital and walked back to the jail. He was surprised how tired he was from the short hike. He dropped into a chair and wiped sweat from his face.

Downes stared at him without expression. Kirk said, "What about the horses, my gear, and my painting?"

"Mindy took care of everything," Downes said shortly.

"What are you going to do about Cowley and Weeb?"

"What can I do? They claim they were just hurrahing you, that they had no intention to let you actually hang. Nobody can prove otherwise."

Kirk put his hands on his knees and leaned forward.

"Marshal, that's a downright lie—and you know it. If you wanted to, you could take them to court on my charge or Mindy's. Maybe Cowley could talk his way out of trouble, but making him take the time would make one more thing galling him."

"Is that what you're staying around for—to gall Cowley?"

"One of these days," Kirk said, "he's going to lose that self-control of his. When he does, he's going to make a mistake."

"When he does, he's going to start a war in Snowy Valley," Downes snapped. He stood up. "I won't waste my time or Judge Breen's by charging Cowley or Weeb—not on your evidence or Mindy's. Now get out of here; I have work to do."

Kirk rose slowly and went to the door. "I hope I don't stop being a man when I get older," he said bitterly. He walked into the sunshine, not looking back.

Mindy's was fairly quiet at this hour, with only two customers sipping beer in the big room. He nodded to Tim O'Shane, the bartender, and looked around for Mindy.

Tim said, "She's upstairs resting for tonight. I'll get her."

"Let her rest," Kirk said, and leaned against the bar.

From the stairs leading to the second floor, Mindy said, "You're the one who needs the rest." She came down quickly and took Kirk's arm. "Can you make it up?"

"I'm fine," he said a little testily.

"I saw you walking across the street," she answered. Her voice was dry.

Suddenly Kirk was too weary to argue. With Mindy's guiding hand, he made the climb to the second floor and down the hall to one of the three rooms she had fitted for the occasional rancher who couldn't make it home on a Saturday night. Kirk pulled off his boots and stretched on the bed with a sigh.

Mindy took a chair and turned it to face him. She sat

down. "I have your saddlebags and painting," she said. "The horses are in my stable behind the Palace."

"I keep getting deeper into your debt," he said.

Mindy smiled. "I don't mind that at all." Her warm chuckle welled up and then faded away. "But you might have a chance to pay off that debt before long. Cowley came in late last night when we were closing up."

Kirk frowned. "How long did he give you to pack up and leave?"

"Five days."

"In four days I fight Weeb," Kirk said. "Maybe Cowley'll change his mind after that."

"Nothing but a bullet or a noose will change Cowley's mind," Mindy said. "He didn't come out and threaten Marshal Downes yesterday after you left, but he made it pretty plain that if he was given any trouble, he'd start a war."

She got up before Kirk could answer. "You're pale. When did you eat last?"

Kirk managed a chuckle. "You sound like a mother hen. I had some broth at the Doc's."

"Broth! That won't put strength back into you." She hurried out. Kirk closed his eyes and fell quickly asleep. He awakened as quickly to the smell of something that set his stomach growling.

It was a thick stew with great chunks of freshly baked bread and a mug of strong coffee. Mindy helped him sit up and watched while he ate. He was surprised at his appetite and he had to resist wolfing the food. Finished, he lay back, started to thank Mindy, and fell asleep again.

It seemed to Kirk that the next two days were a repetition of the first at Mindy's. He ate and slept and woke to eat again. He exercised by walking around the room— a little longer between each sleep. At first, he thought his bruised ribs and kidney would never ease, but finally the soreness began to go away. The third day, he went downstairs at dinner time.

Judge Breen and Lawyer Parker were eating at their usual table but without Cowley this time. Parker motioned Kirk over. He took a chair, nodding his greeting.

"I just thought you should know," the lawyer said, "that Downes was right. He told us the details of what happened the other night. You'd have a hard time making any charge stick against Cowley."

"Are you afraid of his starting a war too?" Kirk asked bluntly.

"Cowley has the trained gunhands," Judge Breen said slowly. "He has two-thirds of the businessmen and half the ranchers afraid to say no to him."

"It's no way for a free man to want to live," Kirk said.

"I've thought of that too," the Judge answered. "But Cowley is no fool, Kirk. He covers his tracks pretty well. He hasn't yet made the mistake that would justify—to my mind—taking legal action against him."

"What good would legal action do—if he fought it with force?"

"Force without legal sanction is one thing," Judge Breen said. "With it, force is something else." He shook his head at Kirk and smiled thinly. "Don't misjudge Downes. He hasn't given up. He isn't backing down. But he's a lawman first. Give him the legal right to go after Cowley and Weeb, and he won't hesitate."

"That's fine," Kirk answered. "If it isn't too late by then." Rising, he nodded and left.

He stood at the bar and sipped a beer. Mindy came up to him. "You look upset."

"The judge and Parker aren't much better than the marshal," he said. He told her of the conversation.

"What are we supposed to do—make Cowley break the law and get caught at it?"

"That was in my mind," Kirk said. "It won't take many more pushes to make him lose his control." He put a hand to his ribs. "In another day or two I just might be ready to do a little pushing."

Mindy started to speak and then moved away as one of her customers signaled from the back of the room. Kirk finished his beer and went back upstairs. He slept and ate and then Ira Moss came to his room.

He grinned at Kirk. "You look in pretty good shape," he said. His grin slipped. "But maybe that ain't going to be enough to do no good."

"What's Cowley up to now?"

Ira sat down and crossed his legs. He thumbed back his hat. "I went to see Carla yesterday to tell her you'd be up and around and back at the meadow to finish the dam in a few days. She told me she'd changed her mind. Now she don't want the dam finished." He snorted. "She wouldn't admit Cowley got to her, but I know dang well he did."

"Did you tell her about the gold horse?"

"She wouldn't talk about Fancher," Ira said. "And when I told her you was bringing the horse soon, she made it pretty plain she didn't want nothing to do with anything Fancher ever touched." He added, "And that old coot of a foreman of hers—Jake Powell—he said if we did bring the gold, he'd run it right off."

"I know Jake," Kirk said. "He wouldn't." He shook his head. "Carla will get over her hurt and change her mind after a month or so. Meantime, I guess we can keep the gold in your pasture."

Kirk got up. "We can do it now. I need the exercise."

He was amused to see the way Ira watched him as he saddled the roan and tied a lead rein to his saddle for the gold. He found that his muscles were a little stiff, but most of the soreness was gone, and getting into the fresh air was pleasant.

On the way, he told Ira about his conversation with Judge Breen and Lawyer Parker. Ira grunted. "A man in the judge's position can't do much else but see it that way. So I'd say we got to make Cowley get caught breaking the law."

"You and Mindy think a lot alike," Kirk commented. "If you find a way to get Cowley to hang himself, let me know."

"Get Cowley riled enough and he'll do it to himself," Ira said.

"That's the way I figure it," Kirk agreed. "That's why I can't put off fighting Weeb. I challenged him a week ago tomorrow night."

Ira turned to gape at him. "You're crazy! You can't fight Weeb so soon. He'll whip you sure—maybe even kill you with his fists."

"No," Kirk said. "I'm as ready as I'll ever be, and I don't think Weeb can whip me—not the way he did ten years ago."

Ira grumbled deep in his throat. "What does Mindy say about it?"

"It seems I haven't got around to mentioning it yet," Kirk said.

"Maybe you better," Ira said dryly, "seeing as the fight can't take place nowhere but her Palace."

"I wouldn't do that to Mindy," Kirk objected.

"And where else in town can you fight Weeb fair and square? Any other place'll be full of Weeb's bully boys standing with their guns out. And if you won, you'd still lose."

"What's to keep them out of Mindy's?"

"You seen Mindy handle a gun. You seen me and my old Sharps. You answer that."

Kirk chuckled. "We'll leave it up to Mindy."

"You know her," Ira chuckled. "She'll most likely find

a way to sell tickets." His mirth drained away. "And what happens if you lose the fight? Lose it fair and square?"

"Then I won't have much choice," Kirk said. "I'll pack up and leave. But if I win, a lot of people are going to stop being so scared of Weeb. And that means they'll stop being scared of Cowley."

Ira said dourly, "See that you win. If you don't, you won't be alone when you ride out of Snowy Valley. Not after the way Mindy and me stood up to Cowley at the pass."

X

A FEW HOURS before the fight, Kirk ate a light dinner. Then he went upstairs and stretched out on the bed. He was staring at the ceiling, working over his plan for the fight, when Ira came in.

"I passed the word all around," he said. "You can bet there'll be a mob in here tonight."

"Did Weeb get the word, I wonder?"

Ira chuckled. "Oh, he got it. One-eye was in Grogarty's when I stopped off there. As soon as I got through my spiel, he lit out on his horse. Weeb'll be here sure as the good Lord made people like him to test people like you."

Kirk flexed his hands into fists. "I don't think I'll wait for the Lord to come and help me—not tonight," he said. He started to say more and broke off as a hard rap came at the door.

"Gannon, it's Downes."

"Door's open," Kirk said.

The marshal came in and looked sourly down at him. "There'll be no fight tonight between you and Weeb—or ever, as long as I have a say."

"Since when have you ever tried to stop a fair fight—and this one'll be fair."

75

"The fight doesn't worry me," Downes said. "I made that plain enough when you challenged Weeb a week back. But if you win, your life won't be worth a busted horseshoe."

"I can take care of myself, Marshal." Kirk sat up. "That's what worries you, isn't it? Because you know that if Cowley and Weeb really push me, I'll push back just as hard—and maybe harder."

"My job is to keep the peace. You made the challenge, so I'm holding you to blame. I want you riding out of this valley tonight."

"Kirk's no common vagrant!" Mindy said hotly from the open doorway. "You have no right to run him out."

"He's a troublemaker," Downes snapped.

"So am I," Mindy said. "So is Ira. Are you going to run us out for standing against Lex Cowley?"

"I have no say about you. You're property owners. Gannon isn't." He turned and stalked to the door. Mindy stepped aside. "I want you riding in an hour, Gannon," he said. He moved on to the stairs and out of sight.

Ira Moss stroked his chin and grinned. "Mindy, fetch me some ink, paper, and a pen."

She matched his smile with one of her own and moved away. Coming back, she handed Ira the writing materials. While she and Kirk watched, the old man rested the paper on the dresser top and scribbled for a few minutes. He handed the paper to Kirk.

"Give me a dollar," he said.

Kirk pulled a dollar from his pocket and handed it to him. Then he read the paper: "I, Ira Moss, hereby sell one half of the Oval-M Ranch to Kirk Gannon, formerly of Snowy Valley, Oregon, in exchange for one dollar and other considerations—signed Ira Moss, sole owner of the Oval-M, free and clear."

"Tomorrow we'll get Lawyer Parker to draw it all up

fancy," Ira said, "with a survivor clause and everything so it's all legal. But for tonight that'll spike Downes' gun."

"Thanks, old timer," Kirk said, "but why don't we just let this keep until everything is over. Then I'll give you back the paper."

"You'll give me nothing!" Ira screeched. "We made a deal and you got to stick with it. I got me a working partner now. I ain't no fool to let him get loose. So now you got another good reason to whip Weeb."

Kirk laughed. Then he said more soberly, "Downes is right, of course. If I win, Cowley will try to kill me. But trying to do something isn't getting it done." He started for the door and paused. "If I don't win . . ."

"Then you'll have company when you ride out of the valley," Ira said dourly. "Me and Mindy."

When Kirk reached the foot of the stairs, the noise welling up the big room began to dribble away. The tables had been pushed back, leaving a considerable space between the first row and the bar. It seemed to Kirk that all the men in Snowy Valley were at the tables, and all of them were looking at him.

Only one man stood at the bar—Weeb. He had his back to the mirror, his elbows hooked over the mahogany. He saw Kirk and grinned, showing his stained teeth.

"I hear you're looking to fight me, Gannon," he said through the thick silence.

"That was the agreement last week," Kirk answered. "But if you'd rather pick up and ride, I won't stop you."

Weeb scowled at the laughter that greeted this. He took a step forward, thrusting his heavy features at Kirk. "I'm going to tell you for the last time—after I whip you tonight, you're going out of this valley." He looked around. "And those so-called friends of yours that ain't here are going along."

For the first time Kirk realized that Mindy wasn't in

sight and that Ira had not come down the stairs after him. He let none of his surprise at this show in his expression. He said, "Move back, Weeb. I nearly got blown down by that last blast of wind."

"By God—" Weeb grabbed a whiskey glass from the bar, clenched it in one massive fist and rushed at Kirk.

"Hold it right there!" a voice snapped from above.

Weeb jerked to a stop. Everyone looked past Kirk, up the stairs. Mindy stood there, a rifle cradled in one arm. "This is going to be a fair fight. So tell your men to come up and lay their guns on the bar."

"My men ain't here. I don't need nobody to help me whip Gannon."

"There are six L-in-C hands buried in the crowd," Mindy snapped. "They put their weapons on that bar or you forfeit the fight."

Weeb looked like he wanted to argue. Then the front door came open and Ira Moss appeared. He had gone down the back way, Kirk thought, and circled around. He stood now with his old Sharps in his hand.

"Like the lady said," he announced. "This'll be a fair fight."

Weeb said grudgingly, "All right, boys."

Six men worked their way through the crowd and laid their guns on the bar. Tim O'Shane swept them up and put them out of sight. Kirk nodded and moved toward Weeb. "Your gun too," he said softly.

Weeb unbuckled his gunbelt and tossed it to O'Shane. He started for Kirk, his big body swinging at the shoulders like a bear's. His arms hung loose; his fists were like chunks of rock. He grinned again.

Kirk stood and waited, feeling the remaining soreness still in his muscles and remembering back ten years when Weeb had used those fists on him. "Ever do any boxing, Weeb?" he asked pleasantly.

"Why, you going to give me a lesson?"

"I just might," Kirk said. Weeb stopped two feet from him and lifted a heavy arm. "You going to pose or fight?" Kirk demanded.

Weeb lunged forward, swinging his right arm in a powerful sweep that would have crushed Kirk if it had landed. Kirk ducked away, but not as Weeb obviously expected, into the big man's cocked left. Instead he came spinning to face Weeb from the side. He drilled a blow that caught Weeb on the temple, rocking him a little. Weeb swung around and lashed out with both fists.

Kirk caught the left fist on his arm and felt Weeb's power. He took another spinning step and flicked two light, almost glancing blows into Weeb's face. Weeb blinked and then laughed.

"You call them powder puffs hands, Gannon?" He did a little dancing himself and loosed a swing that almost caught the other off balance. Kirk managed to step back in time.

The force of his swing sent Weeb off balance, and Kirk bored in, rapping Weeb twice under the eye before Kirk had to move again. Weeb growled and charged. Kirk moved lightly away, parrying a slashing right and slipping a left over his shoulder. He caught Weeb once on the mouth and once under the eye before he retreated.

"Hold still and fight!" Opie yelled shrilly from the crowd.

Kirk paid no attention. His eyes moved constantly, noting Weeb's way of handling his body, his feet and his arms. He caught the way Weeb signaled with his shoulders and a movement of the head when he was ready to throw a big punch. He let Weeb move him toward the bar. It was in his mind to make Weeb charge and then duck aside, letting Weeb ram the bar with his big chest. He ducked a right and landed a blow that cracked Weeb's lip. Weeb hammered out a left. Kirk stepped back and felt the bar catch him across the back.

I misjudged the space, he thought. Before he could work free, Weeb was there, his mouth split in a grin of triumph and his eyes gleaming. Now Kirk had no room to go backward and he could only hold off Weeb's rock-hard fists with his forearms and with sharp sideways movements. He blocked three solid blows before the fourth caught him on the temple. It sent him spinning sideways. He grabbed for the bar for support, missed, and went to his knees.

"Finish him off!" an excited voice called.

Weeb moved with surprising speed for his size; he reached down to pull Kirk up by the shirt. Kirk chopped at the hand that gripped him, but his strength hadn't come back yet, and Weeb hauled him easily to his feet.

Weeb opened his fingers, freeing Kirk. He reached out and hit Kirk in the ribs with a left, in the stomach with a right. Kirk twisted away. Weeb's next blow caught him on the temple again, and for the second time he went to his knees.

Weeb stepped forward, one heavy leg swinging for his unprotected face. Someone shouted a warning. The sound changed to a cheer as Kirk leaned to one side, caught Weeb's ankle and jerked. Weeb lifted up and slammed down on his back, raising dust from the floor. Kirk got to his feet and backed to the bar, resting against it while he waited for Weeb to get up.

"Stomp him, Gannon!" a voice called. "Stomp him good."

Kirk shook his head and waited. Weeb pulled breath back into his body and climbed to his feet. He shook his head like a bear throwing water from its face. He found Kirk waited and he stared, his lips drawn back in anger.

"You heard the rules," Kirk said. "This is to be a fair fight. The next time you try using your boot on me, I'll jerk it off and ram it down your throat. Now start fighting!"

Weeb cursed him and rushed, swinging in wild anger. Kirk slipped away, came about and hit Weeb twice under the eye. Weeb slammed against the bar, turned and rushed again. Kirk let a tight grin cross his mouth. As long as Weeb fought this way, out of control, it was only a matter of time. He flicked out his fists again, working on the flesh under Weeb's eyes and on his loose-hanging lips. After a time, Weeb began to come in more slowly, shuffling his feet, seeking an opening.

But now he was beginning to peer for Kirk as his eyes puffed up and threatened to close. Kirk kept coming at him, cutting with his fists and then dancing away. The crowd began to hoot, obviously enjoying the sight of Weeb being outfought, being played with like an awkward boy.

"Stand still and fight," Weeb growled.

Kirk hit him once in the mouth and twice over the eyes. Blood flowed into Weeb's bushy eyebrows and began to drip down. He shook his head and swung it, seeking Kirk. Obligingly, Kirk stood still. Weeb roared and stumbled toward him.

Kirk began to maneuver him now. He poked out his fist, making Weeb turn aside and back until finally he was pressed against the bar. Kirk began to twist his fists as he lashed at Weeb's face—in and out. Weeb tried to move forward and was jolted back with a hard blow to the mouth. He roared again and lifted both arms, swinging them aimlessly, blindly.

Kirk shifted his attack to Weeb's body. It was like hitting corrugated iron, he realized as he went to work on Weeb's big biceps. Weeb began to wince as he tried to lift his arms. Finally he stood with his arms hanging and his face unprotected. Kirk stepped back.

"Does someone want to take this thing out of here or do I have to kill him first?"

Weeb began to sag at the knees. Kirk moved forward and propped him up, holding him almost casually. The crowd hooted with joy. Kirk felt Weeb's weight grow heavy and he stepped aside, drawing his arm away. Weeb took a pace forward, tried to turn, and then crashed like a felled tree. He lay still.

Led by Opie and Red, the six L-in-C hands came forward. Opie bent over his protector and then glared at Kirk. "You ain't heard the last of this, Gannon. By damn, you'll be in hell before another week's out."

"Why, you getting lonesome there, Opie?"

The crowd roared with laughter. Opie signaled for the other men to take the big body, and he led the way out past Ira, still standing with his Sharps.

Mindy came down the steps. "Push the tables back where they belong, please, gentlemen. And have a drink on the house."

She laughed at the cheer that went up and hurried to where Kirk stood. "Are you all right?"

He nodded. "You can't afford to go giving drinks away," he teased. "It'll cut into the money you got for selling all those tickets."

Mindy laughed with him. "Right now," she said, "I could give this place away and never know it. Thank God you're all right!"

He looked down at her. "It means that much to you to be able to stay here?"

"You mean that much to me," she corrected him softly.

Kirk reached out and touched her hand. Then he said, "I'd like a beer for my drink. I'm a little thirsty."

Ira Moss trotted up. "Did he hurt you?"

"At first," Kirk said. "I'll have bells in my ears for a while." Tim O'Shane slid the beer to his hand. He gulped it down. "Right now, I'd like to get some rest. I have the feeling I'm going to be busy the next few days."

He started for the stairs and stopped as a familiar voice said, "Hold it, Gannon."

Sighing, he turned. "What is it, Marshal?"

"I gave orders you weren't to fight. I told Ira you were riding out of here. I meant it; you go tonight."

Ira Moss came forward. "Now, Marshal, you told me not two hours ago you couldn't really run property owners out."

"Property? Gannon doesn't even have a job—a reason to be here any more—let alone property. Or are you claiming your father's spread now?" He looked at Kirk.

Shaking his head in answer to the question, Kirk took the contract Ira had drawn up and handed it to Downes. The marshal read it, his lips thinning.

He slammed the paper back into Kirk's hand. "You're a pair of damn fools," he snapped. "And remember this, Ira. It'll take more than that dollar he gave you to bury him—after Weeb and Cowley get done."

Swinging around, he marched away.

XI

Cowley stood by the big window in his parlor and stared at the four men facing him. He nodded to Weeb. "You look terrible. Can you see yet?"

"Enough," Weeb said thickly. "Gannon didn't hurt me much. He just marked me up."

"That's all he was trying to do," Cowley said. "Mark you so everyone would know that he stands taller than the L-in-C." He smashed a fist into the palm of his other hand. "I've had enough of Gannon. Between him and that fool Arthur, I'm getting nowhere right now."

He took a deep breath. "The mail stage will be in day after tomorrow, and Arthur's letter is sure to be on it. That means we have to do something in a hurry."

Opie said shrilly, "Fooling with the mails ain't too good an idea. It ain't like pushing the marshal around here."

Cowley glared him to silence. "Who said anything about

fooling with the mails? Let the letter come. But when it does, I want to be sure Downes isn't in any shape to read his copy."

"We can't go gunning down the marshal!" Weeb rumbled.

"Shut up and listen," Cowley said. He thrust his head forward. "Why should we have to gun down the marshal when we can get someone else to do it—or make it look like someone else did it?"

Nobody spoke. He went on, "You heard that Ira Moss sold a half interest in his spread to Gannon. All right, what happens to it if Moss should up and die?"

"If it's like most sales here," Weeb said thoughtfully, "the survivor gets the ranch." He twisted his puffed lips in a grin. "And that's Gannon! By God, if Ira Moss should get gunned down and there was witnesses to say Gannon done it, then Downes is bound to haul him in and lock him up."

"That's right," Cowley said with a satisfied nod. "And what would happen if Gannon suddenly had to get out of jail in a hurry—to help Mindy fight a fire at her place, say. What do you think Gannon would do?"

"Given half a chance, he'd bull his way out," Weeb said.

"And if Downes happened to get trampled just then, who's to say Gannon didn't do it? An accused murderer doesn't worry too much about who he hurts when he's trying to get free."

"You could make a story like that stick?"

"I can—if we time everything right." He jammed a fist into his palm again. "Now here's the way we'll do it. If Red saw right, Gannon left town today and rode back to the Oval-M."

"I saw right," Red rumbled. "I was in the trees when he came by on his roan, riding watchdog for Moss with the freight wagon. I heard Gannon say he was going to the meadow later."

"He's trespassing," Opie said shrilly. "We tell Carla and—"

"Forget that," Cowley snapped. "Let him trespass. Who's going to know he's at the meadow—when witnesses will be claiming he was busy gunning down Moss? Red, you ride back and keep an eye on the Oval-M. As soon as Gannon rides off and leaves Moss, make your move. Take One-eye and Corvo with you. And be sure you leave no sign—unless it's Gannon's."

One-eye and Red moved to the door. Weeb watched them go. He chuckled. "I got to hand it to you," he said to Cowley. "If this works, you won't have no more trouble with Gannon."

"It'll work," Cowley snapped. "It has to work. I'm going to own this valley inside of two more days if I have to shoot down half the people in it!"

The afternoon sun warmed Kirk as he threw his saddle on the gold horse. Ira Moss came from the kitchen of the small ranch house and watched him.

"Exercising the gold?"

"I'm going to ride him to the meadow," Kirk said. "The roan threw a shoe."

"Unless you want me there at the meadow," Ira said, "I'll take him in to get a new shoe. I got to see Lawyer Parker anyway."

Kirk tightened the cinch, waited until the gold let out his breath, and then took it up another notch. "You going to back out on our contract?"

Ira laughed. "Downes sure wishes I would. He's been shivying Parker, claiming my selling to you was a trick. Parker said I'd be smart to swear out an affidavit that you didn't force me into the sale or some such fool thing."

"I'm surprised Parker gave you the advice," Kirk said. "He and Judge Breen didn't seem to think much more of my staying in the valley than Downes does."

"I told Parker off about that," Ira said in his feisty way.

"I asked him if he'd rather live under Cowley's thumb without having put up a fight or if he'd rather be proud of himself. He looked kinda thoughtful, so maybe I done some good."

Kirk nodded and climbed into the saddle. "I'll get back before you and fix supper. Leave the roan if you have to. I can pick him up later."

Nodding again, he trotted the gold out of the yard and around the house. He had two ideas in mind—to see if any of his tools or equipment had been disturbed in the past week and to find a reason he could use to get Carla Belden to change her mind and let him finish the dam. He rode quickly, wanting to reach the meadow as soon as possible. He was well out of earshot when a gun cracked a short distance north of the Oval-M.

Ira Moss was riding slowly on his paint, letting the roan pick its sore-footed way along the trail. He crossed the creek that marked the northern boundary of the Oval-M, thought about taking the valley road, and decided to stay on the hill trail for the sake of the roan.

He hadn't gone twenty yards past the creek when he heard the crack of a dry branch under a hoof. He pulled his rifle from the boot and turned to his right. He was lifting the rifle when the shot caught him in the body. Its force lifted him from the saddle and slammed him to the ground.

The paint leaped forward and the roan went in the opposite direction. The lead rein broke and the roan galloped into the timber on the left side of the trail. The paint, snorting in terror, raced north. Ira lay motionless where he had fallen, his Sharps under his body.

From behind a screen of bushes, Red said, "One-eye, go see if he's dead. And watch you don't leave no sign. Take a branch and brush out your footprints."

"What about the prints the roan left?" One-eye asked. "What'll Downes make of them?"

"Seeing that's Gannon's horse, I'd say he'll make plenty," Red said. He guffawed. "Hell, it's ready made, ain't it? When Corvo and me gallops into town to tell the marshal what we seen and he comes back and finds the sign from Gannon's horse here—" He laughed again.

One-eye grinned and then slipped onto the trail. He went up to Ira and bent down, putting a hand close to the old man's slack mouth. Straightening up, he backed away, wiping out his boot tracks with whisks of a pine branch. Once in the bushes, he nodded to Red. "If he ain't dead, he's the only man I ever seen who could live without breathing."

"Good enough," Red said. "You head for the ranch. Corvo and I'll find the body and go skyhooting for town." Laughing, he moved away toward his horse.

Ira Moss remained motionless, wondering how he was able to hear all this talk when he should be dead. *But,* he figured, *no dead man had ears good enough to hear Red and One-eye talking not fifteen feet away, and no dead man could hurt the way I do in the brisket.*

When One-eye came up to him, he held his breath and let his body lie loosely, hoping to fool the L-in-C rider and knowing that if he failed, One-eye would shoot him a second time. When One-eye retreated to the bushes, he let out his breath and sucked in fresh air carefully, not wanting him or Red to see his body move. He listened to the rest of their talk and slowly began to understand what they were up to. He wondered whether he could stand and, if so, whether he could ride.

He was working to gather strength to force his pain-shot body out of the dirt when he heard horses coming. He let himself lie loose again as he heard Red's rumbling chuckle.

Red cried, "Look there, Corvo! I'd say there's been a

killing. And ain't that Gannon riding hell-bent off into the timber?"

"It sure is," Corvo answered. "I say we better ride for the marshal."

They galloped on, Red's laugh flowing back to reach Ira's ears. He lay until the last hoofbeat had faded and then he made himself stand. He was as sick with anger as he was with pain and he forced himself to put a rein on his temper. He looked around, wondering how far up the trail the paint had gone. He spotted the roan with its lead rein tangled in a thicket. Slowly he made his way to the horse.

"Hoof or no hoof, you got to carry me to town," he said. "And mighty quick." He pulled the roan free, grasped its mane, and with all the strength left in his body, hauled himself onto the horse's back. He could feel blood warm against his skin and he looked down at the growing stain at the side of his shirt.

"Hell," he said aloud, "I'm leaking like a tore-up water-bag." He felt blackness closing in, and he knew he could never make the long ride to Snowy. He thought he might make the meadow and at least warn Kirk of what had happened. He turned the roan in that direction, buried his fingers in the horse's thick mane, and kicked it into motion.

He kept slipping as consciousness dribbled away from him. Each time, he came back to life and pulled himself upright. The direction of his pulling was the direction the roan wanted to take and Ira used a good deal of strength forcing it back onto the trail. At the junction with the road to the valley, he slipped again and when he righted himself the roan was heading down that way. Ira thought fuzzily that he shouldn't be riding downhill, but his mind and body weren't up to working out the puzzle and he slumped forward, letting the horse have its head.

The roan reached the valley road. Not being told to turn, it plowed straight on, down the twin ruts that led to the B-Bar. Ira lifted his head, saw the familiar ranch house swimming into his vision, and swore. But he had no choice, he realized. He lacked the strength to ride much farther than this. Tightening his grip, he kicked the roan to a faster pace, sending it limping more quickly up the road. The jouncing sent knives of pain slashing through him. The blackness came more strongly now and he had nothing left to fight it with.

He wasn't aware of riding into the yard behind the B-Bar, nor of Carla Belden's cry as she rushed out to him. He didn't feel the strong hands lift him out of the saddle and take him into the house. He just lay bleeding.

Kirk returned from the meadow satisfied that nothing had been touched, unsatisfied that he hadn't come up with a good argument to use on Carla Belden. It was growing dusky and he lit some lamps and set about getting supper, figuring that Ira would be along shortly. He had the stove going and water heating for coffee when he heard a horse coming quickly into the yard. He glanced out of the window, surprised to see Marshal Downes. He went to the door and opened it.

Downes stepped from his horse. "Pack your war-bag, Gannon." His gun came out. "Put your .44 down easy like and get ready to ride."

Kirk stared at him. "Marshal, we've been all over this. You have no legal right to run me out."

"I'm running you only one place—to jail."

"On what charge?"

"Killing Ira Moss," Downes snapped. "And don't give me any argument. Save that for Judge Breen tomorrow. Two witnesses claim they saw you and they swore out the charge. So I'm taking you in."

Kirk felt as if Weeb's fist had buried itself in his middle. "Ira's dead?"

"So Red and Corvo claim," Downes said. "They say you shot him down by the fork that leads down to the valley. When I got there, I didn't see anything but blood." He sounded less angry and almost dubious now. "But I got no choice, Gannon. They made the charge. All I do is act on it."

"L-in-C men! And you'd listen to them at a time like this?" Kirk swore and broke off. "Marshal, maybe Ira wasn't dead, only wounded. He could be crawling in the timber somewhere, looking for help. He could be lying—"

"I have two men scouring for him right now," Downes said. "I didn't come alone. Now do what I told you."

Kirk drew his gun and handed it butt first to Downes. Then he went inside, doused the fire, packed his war-bag, and returned. Saddling the gold, he mounted. They started for town.

Downes said, "Where's your roan?"

"He threw a shoe. Ira was taking him to the blacksmith for me."

Downes pursed his lips thoughtfully. "I saw the roan's tracks. He looked to have been limping some, but he wasn't empty. Someone was riding him. Toward the valley," he added.

"What about Ira's horse?"

"He came snorting into town before Red and Corvo, running like devils was after him."

"My guess is that Ira was riding the roan," Kirk said. "Why don't we follow the trail to the valley and see?"

"I got a job to do," Downes said shortly. "Just keep going for town."

Kirk said slowly, "Marshal, you're playing right into Cowley's hands. I say he had Ira shot and told Red and Corvo to claim I did it. He's not fool enough to think he can make the charge stick—and that means he wants me out of the way for a little while. Maybe just for tonight.

"Maybe he wants you out of the way too, figuring you'll keep busy guarding me."

Downes grunted. Kirk went on, "I say we'd better find out just what Cowley is planning—and when it's going to happen."

"I'm the law here. I'll take care of whatever trouble comes."

"Maybe," Kirk said. "But you take care of it after it happens. And one of these times you're going to be too late. I think that time is right now."

XII

KIRK STOOD in a puddle of moonlight and looked through his cell door at the dimly-lighted jail office. Downes had fed him, written out a paper, and then had turned down the lamp and left. Kirk frowned. He hadn't expected the marshal to walk away, leaving him alone like this.

And he hadn't expected Downes to leave the jail keys lying on his desk, not five feet from the cell door. Kirk wondered if the marshal was trying to set a trap. He shook his head. Downes wasn't that clever—or that type of man.

Kirk shrugged. Whatever reason Downes had, he wasn't going to pass up his chance to get free and hunt for Ira. As long as there was a chance the old man still lived, he wanted to try to find him. Quickly now, he went to his cot and took it apart until he had one of the long side rails free.

He moved back to the door, carefully pushed the rail through the bars until he could pull the keys from the desk with one end. When they hit the floor, he worked them toward him until he could reach out and pick them up. That done, he unlocked the cell door, replaced the iron rail, and then went into the room and put the keys back. He returned to the cell, leaving the door shut but not locked.

"I'll give it an hour," he said aloud. If the marshal was planning a trap, he should know about it by then. He sat on the cot, listening to the night sounds of town—the leaving of Mindy's last customers, the raucous laugh of a drunk down near Grogarty's. Then he heard a sound that made him stiffen. Silence had settled over Snowy, and through it he could hear the pad of muffled hoofs.

He located them as across the street and just south of Mindy's. Leaving the cell, he moved to the curtained front window. Kneeling, he drew one edge of cloth aside and peered out. The moon was full and it threw hard light on the scene across the street, on the five shadowy riders dropping from their horses to move softly toward Mindy's Palace.

Kirk saw a match flare and then a torch caught fire, throwing its yellow light vividly for an instant. Opie's ferret features were briefly outlined. He passed the torch to another man and trotted quickly away.

Kirk swung from the window and looked around for his gun. It was not in sight. He went hurriedly through the marshal's desk. Finally, cursing his own stupidity, he caught up the keys and opened the gunrack on the wall. Arming himself with a .44 and a carbine, he moved out the side door and down the valley to the corner with the cross street. When he crossed the main street, he was on the far side of the building from the L-in-C hands.

A glance upward showed him a light in Mindy's apartment, another in O'Shane's. Quickly now he tried the door leading into the ladies' dining room. The latch refused to yield. Stepping back, Kirk threw his weight forward, driving his shoulder against the door frame. It creaked but held. He lunged again. The third time the lock ripped loose. He plunged into the darkened room, caromed off a table and righted himself. A door slammed above and light appeared beneath a door across the room as someone came downstairs with a lamp.

Kirk worked his way to the door, opened it, and stepped into the bar. He saw O'Shane with a gun in his hand. "It's Kirk Gannon," he called. "Cowley's crew is firing the building."

O'Shane ripped out an Irish curse, left the lamp and raced up the stairs again. Kirk followed as Mindy appeared, a heavy robe over her nightdress. "We can see them from the south windows," Kirk said quickly. He opened the door to the room he had spent so many days in and crossed to the window.

Throwing up the sash, he leaned out. The torch danced below him, but to its left and right flame licked at small piles of dry grass pushed against the dry walls of the big building. Torchlight showed Kirk two men working to set another grass fire against a wall toward the rear. Leveling the carbine, he took quick aim and fired. One of the men lifted from his haunches and flung himself sideways to lie kicking. The other stayed double and tried to run out of the flickering light.

Kirk cut his leg out from under him and then jerked back as a gun cracked, sending lead whistling past his head. From another upstairs window a handgun opened up, and beyond it came the sharper crack of a rifle. A man cried out in pain and surprise. Then rifle fire raked the windows, forcing the defenders to pull back, giving the wounded men the chance to get to their horses.

Hoofs hammered in the night. Kirk ran to the window again and leaned out. The riders were racing south. He fired twice and missed. Holstering the handgun, he ran downstairs, calling O'Shane's name.

"They've gone," Kirk shouted. "Get some water." He could hear the crackle as the fire began to take hold of the dry, wooden wall. Thin ribbons of smoke drifted into the big, downstairs room. Swearing at his lack of knowledge of the place, Kirk caught up the lamp and stumbled into the kitchen. He found a bucket, filled it at the sink pump, and hurried to the back door.

Mindy had dressed. Taking the lamp from his hand, she opened the door for him. "I sent O'Shane to spread the alarm," she said briefly. "I'll bring more water."

Outside, Kirk raced around the corner and splashed the contents of the bucket on the nearest fire. It had gained enough headway now that he was only able to slow down the flames. Ripping off his shirt, he swung it head high, beating at the fire, choking as the wind he created sent smoke billowing around him.

He caught a glimpse of Mindy coming with two buckets. Turning, he caught one and threw it against the flames. She emptied the second. Kirk panted, "Get something to pull the fire from the bottom of the walls." He went back to beating at the tongues of flames climbing the wall.

A pitchy board exploded, driving him back briefly. He felt the heat blistering his face, A roaring filled his ears, and it was some time before he realized the sound came from men rushing to help.

Kirk was staggering from exhaustion when a hand caught his arm and pulled him away from the wall. He jerked free and slapped at the wood with the remnants of his shirt.

A voice said, "The fire's all but out."

Kirk stopped and dropped to the ground. After a moment he lifted his head and focused his eyes, tearing from the smoke and heat. He saw Lawyer Parker.

"And you're supposed to be in jail," Parker said with thin humor. He nodded to his left. "Downes is over there."

"Thanks," Kirk said. Drawing to his feet, he moved as quickly as his weariness allowed around to the rear and inside the building. He climbed the stairs and went into the bath near his former room. He washed down with water from the ewer, dried himself, and looked at the strands of cloth that had once been his shirt.

Knuckles hit the door panel. "Kirk?" It was Mindy. "Are you all right?"

"I would be if I had a shirt."

She laughed. "I'll get one of O'Shane's."

He went out, following her down the hallway. O'Shane's shirt was a little tight across the shoulders and tent-sized in the middle, but it covered him. Tucking it in, he looked at Mindy with red-rimmed eyes. "I'll need a horse," he said. "Downes put the gold in the livery."

"You can't go anywhere; you've swallowed enough smoke to cure meat. You need sleep."

"Downes will see to that—if he catches me," Kirk said. "He did all he could for me earlier. He couldn't turn his back on me with others watching. Besides, I have to find Ira."

Mindy nodded. "I heard. I'll change and go with you."

"No, you've got work to do here. Just lend me a horse."

"Help yourself," she said quietly. "But where are you going to sleep? Where will you eat?"

"I can go back to the Oval-M and risk the marshal coming there," Kirk said. "But I don't think he'll bother for a while. The fire will keep him busy."

"You told O'Shane it was L-in-C men. Can you be sure?"

"I saw Opie," Kirk said. "With luck, we'd have three of them still here. Only I shot to stop them, not to kill."

The tightness in his voice made Mindy look closely at his fire-scorched face. "You're going to do more than look for Ira, aren't you? You're going to Cowley's."

"Tomorrow," Kick said. "This has gone far enough. If the marshal and the rest of the people in this valley can't see what Cowley will do next, then they'll have to be shown."

She started to say something and then turned away. Kirk readied himself to go. "How bad is the damage?"

"Nothing I can't repair. Most of it was on the outside, but there's a lot of smoke downstairs."

"I smell it," he said dryly. Reaching out, he touched her hand, caught her brief smile, and then hurried away.

Mindy called, "Don't try to fight Cowley alone!" but Kirk had gone.

XIII

By DAWN Kirk admitted to himself that he was gaining nothing by hunting for Ira Moss in the dark. He had scoured the places he thought most likely and had found nothing. He rode the weary horse to the Oval-M, stabled the animal and went inside.

He risked a fire long enough to make a pot of strong coffee and to cook himself some breakfast. That done, he returned to the barn to find that the horse had finished his oats. Saddling up again, Kirk put the animal on the trail.

"We'll go take a look up by the junction," he said. "Maybe the marshal didn't stomp out all the roan's tracks."

The horse plodded on, too tired to argue.

The sun was edging the eastern mountains when Kirk reached the spot where he judged Ira had been shot. Even now, there was an ugly dark spot staining the pale dirt of the trail.

Getting out of the saddle, he bent and examined the ground. Despite the marshal and his men having ridden over the area, he could still see the sign he sought. Slowly, he constructed a picture of what might have happened.

Ira had been riding, leading the roan. A shot drove him out of the saddle and sent the horses galloping off. He found the timber where the roan had crashed, become tangled, and stood waiting to be released. *One of the drygulchers,*

Kirk guessed, *had come and looked at the body and gone away again. Then Ira had got to his feet, found the roan, and crawled on.* Turning, Kirk made his way into the bushes on the far side of the trail.

He found what he expected—broken twigs, a heavy boot print in damp soil, an empty cartridge case, and the spot where the horses had been tied. Going back to the trail, he started following the prints of the limping roan, as he led the tired horse.

He followed the sign down the trail to the valley road and there he lost it in a welter of prints and where the ground became hard and stony. He climbed into the saddle and rode back a short distance. Turning, he stared over the valley floor at the smoke rising from the L-in-C house ahead and a bit to the left. There was more smoke coming from the B-Bar at an angle on his right.

"Ira got this far," Kirk said aloud. He patted the horse as it bobbed its head. "Now if he had the strength, he would have ridden for Carla's place. But if he didn't, then Cowley's men could have picked him up."

He remained thoughtful a moment and then checked the handgun in his holster and the carbine in his saddle boot. "That's as good a reason as any to go to Cowley's," he told the horse. "But we'll take the long way around. I'm not the type Cowley likes having ride up to his front door."

Laughing tiredly at his own humor, Kirk put heels to the horse, sending it back toward the Oval-M.

Some of the townsmen worked through the night, helping Mindy and O'Shane clean up and making sure the last of the fire was out. With daylight, the marshal went into the vacant field next to the Palace and tried to read the sign of the five horses.

He came back in to find Mindy serving flapjacks and coffee to the weary, drawn men. "They rode in with sacks over the horses' hoofs all right," he said. "I found the sacks. They don't tell me anything."

"Kirk claims he recognized Opie," Mindy said. She had said it before but Downes seemed not to have heard her. Now he had to respond as the others in the room looked at him.

"Gannon isn't in much of a position to talk," Downes said. "I found the tracks of the horse you lent him." He scowled. "I don't cotton to a man taking the law into his own hands."

"I can't see that he's had much choice," Mindy said bluntly and went to the kitchen.

Downes followed her. "I know what you're thinking about me," he said quietly. "But what I do, I do because I'm the law. It isn't always the way I'd do if I wasn't marshal."

"Then resign," Mindy snapped, "if you can't stand yourself this way."

He flushed. "I'm just trying to say that I can guess what Gannon's up to. And if he goes to Cowley's alone, he'll get himself killed. And that won't solve anything. I need help—to find him and stop him from getting himself shot."

"How—by arresting him again?"

"If I have to. But maybe it won't come to that. Maybe he'll have found something that'll give me a reason to go and get Cowley."

"He went hunting for Ira," Mindy said. "He was going to Cowley's today." She added, "Find him, Marshal; keep him from fighting Cowley by himself."

She turned away and hurried upstairs. Changing into her riding clothes, she picked up her gun and went out by the rear door. Downes and his horse were gone and she hurried to the stable and saddled her horse. Putting her gun into the saddle boot, she rode south.

"It isn't that I don't trust you, Marshal," she said aloud. "It's just that I'll feel better if I find Kirk first."

Kirk cut over to the Oval-M and roped a fresh horse from the pasture. Then he rode along the far edge of the valley to the east side, where he began to angle north. At the edge of Cowley's land, he stopped to take a long look. He saw no one; nothing moved but a few head of cattle grazing on hay stubble. Quickly, he sent the horse forward, pulling up finally in a stand of cottonwoods set at the rear of Cowley's house. Leaving the horse, he made another survey and then stepped boldly from the trees and across a strip of hoof-pounded dirt to a point directly under the kitchen window. The sight of smoke from the chimney and the smell of coffee drifting out the open window had brought him here. He nodded in satisfaction as he heard Cowley's sharp voice and Weeb's deep rumble from just inside.

Cowley said, "The next time you're told to do a job, go yourself."

"I wasn't in no shape," Weeb said. "Besides, it's the kind of work Opie does good. I gave him them new men so's they wouldn't be recognized and told him to stay out of sight. But when he found Gannon was in jail, he got cocky."

"I hope he followed today's orders," Cowley said angrily.

"I seen to that," Weeb said. "The whole crew is bunched in three places in the east hills, the way you said. There ain't nobody here but you and me—and Red and One-eye, of course." He chuckled. "They're sitting out in the barn just hoping Gannon will try to come here so's they can throw down on him."

Kirk had a sudden sinking feeling that in his eagerness he had overlooked something. He turned slowly now and nodded. He had guessed right; less than twenty feet away were Red and One-eye.

"Reach for the edge of the roof, Gannon," Red said in a loud voice. Kirk reached. He heard a stir from inside and then a gun muzzle pressed against his neck.

"You want him inside alive, Lex, or outside dead?" Weeb said from behind the gun.

"Bring him in—alive," Cowley snapped.

Kirk made no effort to break free—not with guns in front of him and one at his neck. He went quietly inside, surrendered his own gun, and then boldly pulled out a chair at one end of Cowley's long kitchen table and sat.

Pulling out his pipe, he began to fill it. "You've got nerve coming here alone," Cowley said.

"I came to tell you to pack up your crew and ride," Kirk said levely. "The marshal and the whole town know it was your men behind the fire last night. It's one thing to attack another rancher. It's another to try to burn out a woman."

"You're trying to tell me that Downes is riding here with a posse?"

Kirk lit his pipe and puffed on it. "You're a lot of things, Cowley, but you're no fool. And it would take a fool to think anything else." He lounged back. "And I wouldn't call it a posse. From the talk I heard before I rode out, it's going to be more of a mob—a lynching and shooting kind of mob."

"He's crazy," Weeb said. "There ain't a man in town with guts enough to ride out here and face us down."

"There is since everyone saw me whip you," Kirk said. He shrugged as Weeb swore at him. "Downes is no fool either," he added. "He isn't leading a crew just to see them get wiped out. By now, he'll have found that you don't have most of your men here, that you've got them hiding in the hills, waiting to hit if you need to start a range war." He was looking at Cowley as he spoke.

Weeb said, "He's lying!"

"I don't think so," Cowley said. He nodded. "Gannon's right. Downes has just been waiting for a chance like this to get at us. So have Judge Breen and Parker and a good part of the town." He smiled coldly at Kirk. "So we'll leave you alive for a while, Gannon. And if the mob comes, you'll go out and stop them—hold them back long enough for me to get my men down from the hills. If Downes comes alone, I'll turn you over to him."

Weeb gaped at his boss. "Turn Gannon over to Downes? What for?"

"Someone has to get rid of two meddling fools," Cowley snapped. "And what will the townspeople think when they find Downes and Gannon had a shoot-out on the way to jail—and both ended up dead?"

"By God," Weeb said admiringly, "they'll think Gannon tried to get free, shot the marshal, and got himself shot, too. Just like we planned for last night!"

"That's right," Cowley said with satisfaction. "And without a leader, the mob Gannon is threatening us with won't be much.

"One way or another, we're going to own Snowy Valley by tomorrow!"

XIV

MINDY SAT by Ira's bedside at the B-Bar and studied the old man, marveling at the strength he showed. She had changed his bandages and found that his wound was a clean one. Except for loss of blood and shock, he wasn't too badly hurt.

He said querulously to her, "You figure when Kirk couldn't find me, he rode to Cowley's?" He shifted his position on the bed. "If he's there, Jake Powell will find out. He can sneak up on a hungry mountain cat and never get seen."

Carla came in with a tray of coffee. Outside darkness was closing against the windows, and the night's coolness was drifting in. Ira turned irritably to her. "Did you send a man to my place like I said to tell Kirk or the marshal if they come there where I was?"

"I sent Pete," Carla said. "He just got back. Marshal Downes came a while ago. He's been all over the valley and the hills hunting for you or Kirk." She handed the coffee around, her expression worried. "Now he's ridden for Cowley's. After hearing what Pete had to say, he's determined to arrest Cowley and the whole crew for attemped murder."

"That danged fool," Ira muttered. "He's as crazy as Kirk. But at least he won't be hauling Kirk back to jail again."

"He told Pete he had to," Carla said. "He explained that since there's a charge against Kirk, until something is proved one way or the other, both sides have to go to jail."

"And while he's doing that, Cowley'll take over here— and the rest of the valley—without a fight!" Ira said angrily. He set his coffee down. "You females get out of here. I got to get dressed. I got work to do!"

Jake Powell came stumping in wearily. He was a leathery, sun-baked old cowhand with a voice like the rasp of a buzz saw. "Plenty of work," he said. "I got me a good spot under marshal there. Gannon had Cowley worried about a posse coming and the fool marshal said there wasn't none. So now Cowley is going to make it look like Downes was taking Gannon back to jail and they had a shoot-out and killed each other."

He picked up Ira's coffee and gulped at it. "Then he's going to bring his crew down from the hills and take over the valley." He looked at Carla. "And we'll be first."

Mindy watched Carla's expression and thought, *How she's changed her opinion of Cowley!* She wondered if Carla thought differently about Arthur Fancher now, too.

But wisely she mentioned none of this as she drew Carla from the room, leaving Jake Powell to help Ira dress. Carla said worriedly, "Ira can't ride."

"No, but he can lie in a wagon and he can use a gun," Mindy said.

"I can use a gun, too," Carla said. She turned for her room. "I'm going to change into riding clothes."

"Three of us against Cowley and his crew," Mindy said tightly.

Ira came out, helped by Jake Powell. Powell said, "Six of us, not three. Me and Pete and Porky are going along."

"No," Carla said firmly. "I want at least two men to stay and guard the B-Bar."

"And one," Ira said, "to ride himself to town and tell the Judge and Lawyer Parker what's happening." He chuckled, sounding like his old self. "Now wouldn't it surprise Cowley if the judge got up a posse and they come riding to Cowley's." His chuckle died. "If they don't, some of us won't be alive come morning."

Sitting across the kitchen table from Downes, Kirk looked first at him and then at Cowley. "How long are you going to wait before you take us toward town and shoot us, Cowley?"

"After the moon gets high enough," Cowley said. "I don't want my boys fumbling in the dark." He signaled to Weeb. "Go tell Red and One-eye to round up Opie and the others. Have them ride here. And tell them to get back fast. There's work for them to do." His eyes moved to Downes and Kirk.

Weeb said, "You going to let Red and One-eye take care of Gannon and the marshal here? Hell, that's my job."

"I don't care who does it," Cowley said. "Now get moving." Weeb went.

Marshal Downes looked at his gnarled hands resting on the table and then raised his eyes to Kirk, puffing quietly on his pipe. He said nothing. Kirk nodded at him and offered a sour grin. "At least Cowley fed us, Marshal—the last meal for the condemned men."

Downes said, "Judge Breen will know what happened. He'll send to the county seat for the sheriff's posse."

"Breen won't be alive to send for anybody—not by tomorrow night," Cowley said. "You and Gannon couldn't let well enough alone. You had to force me to play my cards. All right, I'm playing them. Inside an hour or better two dozen men—mine, Mike Tindall's miners, and the east hills ranchers—will be here. I'll own the valley by morning and the town by sundown."

Silence fell. Weeb came back. In a little while a horse could be heard riding hard into the yard. Red appeared in the kitchen doorway. "I was heading up to tell Opie when I saw this wagon and horse and rider." He shook his head and guffawed. "Guess who's coming to attack, boss? Carla Belden and Mindy!" He laughed again. "They'll be here in ten—fifteen minutes." He left, and soon they could hear his horse hammering back toward the hills.

Kirk cursed Mindy and Carla silently. He guessed what they were up to, and he had to admire them for it. But he'd rather have admired them knowing they would still be alive tomorrow.

Downes said, "Cowley, there's no need to hurt the women—"

"That depends on what they try to do to me," Cowley said. Rising, he went into his front parlor and stood by the big windows, looking out at the strengthening moonlight.

Kirk moved next to the marshal. "They'll have to give us room to ride in before they shoot us," he said. "They'll have to make it look good enough to fool the town for a time anyway." His vice was low, not carrying to Weeb. He looked over and scowled at them. Kirk continued, "Maybe we can break for it, then Marshal."

"We can die trying," Downes said dryly. He clenched his fists. "If Cowley hurts Carla or Mindy . . ."

He broke off as the creak of a wagon came to their

ears. It was pulling up in front of the house. Kirk rose and went into the parlor. Downes followed and Weeb came quickly behind, to stand close to both of them.

Cowley threw open the front door, letting lamplight spill out and over Carla on the wagon and Mindy in the saddle. "To what do I owe this pleasure?"

Carla dropped the reins and leaped to the ground, disappearing into shadow beside the wagon. Almost at the same instant the small form of Ira Moss popped up like a jack-in-the-box, a rifle leveled at the door.

"Me," he said. "Now lift your hands, Cowley!"

Beside Kirk, Weeb swore and reached for his gun. At the same time, Cowley tried to step back inside and slam the door. Kirk pushed Weeb, spinning him against Downes. "Get his gun, Marshal!" Swinging around, Kirk caught Cowley's arm, gripped it long enough to draw Cowley's .44 from his holster and then he pushed Cowley out onto the veranda.

He heard movement behind him, turned and saw Weeb leap for a door leading to another part of the house. Downes raised his gun, but he was too late. Weeb was gone.

Kirk stepped outside, staying to one side of Cowley and out of the line of fire from Ira's rifle. He said over his shoulder, "Watch out for Weeb, Marshal."

Ira said, "Now let's load this varmint aboard here and mosey to the jail."

Kirk said with a broad grin, "Old timer, I'm not only glad you're alive. I'm glad you're where you are right now! All right, Cowley, get into the wagon." He glanced toward Mindy, sitting quietly on her horse, her carbine across her lap. "Powell went to town for a posse, Kirk. They should be here soon."

"Can you help Ira watch Cowley while the marshal and I get our horses? And keep a lookout for Weeb. He's loose in the house." He added, "We can't wait."

As if his words were a signal, a shot cracked from a front window and slammed into the side of the wagon. Mindy raised her gun and sent two quick shots upward, shattering glass.

"Try that again and I'll put a bullet in Cowley," she called up.

Cowley snapped, "Wait it out, Weeb. The men will be along soon. Send them to town to get me."

Kirk pushed him in the direction of the wagon. "Marshal, can you get our horses? I'm going inside after Weeb."

Downes nodded and moved swiftly around a corner of the house and out of sight. Kirk waited until Cowley was in the wagon, two guns on him, and then he started back into the house. He moved through the downstairs, holding Cowley's gun, but Weeb was not to be found. He was studying the stairs, thinking how easily a man at the top could shoot down when he heard Downes' call his name. Turning, he hurried outside.

"I can't find your horse," Downes said when he saw Kirk. He was on his own leggy animal. "And a big crew is coming from the east. They're almost here."

Kirk trotted to the wagon, handed Carla back up and climbed onto the seat himself. "I'll drive this then," he said. "Let's get riding."

He lifted the reins to start the team. Mindy cried, "Kirk, watch out!" He swung around to see Cowley make a catlike move that sent one arm out to knock Ira's rifle aside. Without slowing, Cowley vaulted over the side of the wagon and ran. Ira swore and moved to fire at Cowley.

Mindy was cut off by Kirk and Carla and now she moved her horse to get past them. Kirk said, "Let him go. He isn't armed. Killing him wouldn't stop the rest of his crew now, anyway."

Mindy reined up, and Kirk started the team. He said,

"Carla, get in the back and brace Ira. We're going to have to make tracks and it'll be a rough ride."

Now he could hear a thunder of hoofs as a good number of riders came racing toward the house. A horse closer to them nickered and then they saw a blur as Cowley's white swept into sight briefly and then disappeared behind the cottonwoods as it headed east to meet the oncoming men.

Downes was ahead and on Kirk's right and suddenly he came riding back. "More coming from the northeast," he said.

Kirk said tightly, "That will be Mike Tindall and his miners. We'll never get around them and make town." He swung the team, making the wagon rock dangerously. "We'll have to try to find someplace to stand them off!"

From the near distance Cowley's voice lifted on the night. "There they go! Stop them!"

Kirk looked back. Between the small group and the bunched riders, there was little more than an eighth of a mile. He slapped the reins over the team. They responded slowly. He called, "Hang on, Ira. It's going to be a rough one from here on."

"You just drive and leave me be!" Ira Moss snapped.

Kirk jerked the whip from its socket and cracked it across the backs of the horses. "Move out! Run!" He cracked the whip again.

And again he swung the team in a sharp turn.

The horses broke and ran at a wild gallop, sending the wagon jouncing over the rough ground. The sudden change of direction had surprised the L-in-C riders momentarily, and Kirk gained precious yards before they wheeled and came thundering toward the small group.

Kirk fought to keep the wagon from tipping. "Mindy, you get ready to take Carla when we reach those trees ahead. Marshal, you go with them. Maybe Ira and I can keep the mob following us while you get away."

"And you," Mindy said in a pleasant voice, "can go to the devil. You can't shoot and drive that team. You need all the guns you can get."

Kirk gave no answer as he fought the team and wagon across a shallow ditch. Ahead loomed a line of trees, planted as a windbreak. He sent the team between two widely spaced trunks, turned onto a narrow road and snapped the whip again. With firmer footing under their hoofs, the team ran faster.

"They're gaining," Mindy cried.

"Hold your fire until you have to shoot," Kirk told her.

Downes came alongside again. "Where the devil are you going, man? You can't go to the B-Bar. Cowley will burn it out if you do."

"A branch off this road goes around the ranch house and into the meadow where I was building the dam," Kirk answered. He snapped the whip again as the team showed signs of slowing.

Even with the smoother road cutting the pitching of the wagon, the ride turned into a nightmare. Every time he glanced back, Kirk saw that Cowley's men were closer. They had fanned out now, forming a wide arc. He could see Cowley on his great white horse in the lead. Weeb wouldn't be far behind, he knew, and Opie close by him.

"They're going to try to circle us," Kirk warned. "Run, you turtles!" He cracked the whip, nipping hide this time. The horses leaped forward, straining at their harness.

The ranch house was to their left and then it was behind them. Ahead, moonlight sparkled on the water of Snowy Creek and fell on the high rock wall cutting the meadow from the valley. Kirk looked back. Cowley and his crews were almost within gunshot.

From one end of the arc of riders a rifle cracked. The bullet whined past Kirk's head and he realized he had misjudged the distance in the moonlight.

"Answer that, Mindy," he called.

She raised her rifle, sighted briefly, and fired. A man in the long, curving line spun off his horse. Two rifles answered, sending lead whining around them. Marshal Downes began shooting. Mindy sent a second shot and then a third. Kirk realized that it was to keep the attackers off balance.

The road began to pitch and he turned his attention to the team, guiding it up the steepening slope and around a tight curve and then down into the dark, swampy meadow. The horses jolted to a stop as their feet struck the mud. Kirk turned. "Ira?"

"If you missed a chuckhole back there, I ain't sure which one," Ira said. He rose, rifle in hand. "You got us here. How do you get us out?"

"We'll get up against the wall," Kirk said, "and behind the big boulder. Maybe we can hold them off until Powell arrives with the townsmen."

His answer was a shot from the east slope. He felt the bullet catch him in the thigh and send him spinning off the wagon to fall into the wet meadow grass. With a cry Mindy was off her horse and alongside him. Kirk staggered to his feet.

"A crease," he said through clenched teeth. "Let's get the horses and wagon up by the wall. We'll get between the wagon and the boulder."

More shots searched them out as they worked through the clinging muck to the comparative safety of the wall. With rock under his feet, Kirk worked quickly. He positioned the wagon, bringing the team behind it along with the other horses. Putting Mindy and Downes on the big boulder and facing the west slope, he set Carla to hold the horses from bolting and joined Ira in the wagon bed.

Flame blossomed from the east slope and Kirk answered it with a snap shot. A man shouted in pain. A hail of lead swept around the wagon now, battering against the side of the box, whining over their heads.

"How many do you reckon there are?" Ira asked tightly.

"Cowley said twenty-five, counting Mike Tindall, his miners, and the hill ranchers," Kirk answered. Shots came from both slopes now. "And I'd say they're all flanking us."

"And how long do you figure we can hold out against that many guns? We ain't got all the ammunition in the Mercantile to hand," Ira said.

"We can hold out until they decide to make a charge," Kirk answered. "When that happens—it'll be all over."

XV

THEY COULD hear more horses and riders arriving on both slopes. The sporadic shooting fell off abruptly and Cowley's voice lifted through the sudden silence.

"Don't be fools," he called. "Surrender and we'll let all of you ride out of the valley."

"Dead or alive?" Ira Moss called mockingly.

Cowley's answer was a shouted, "Now!" Before the echoes of his voice faded, guns opened up from both slopes, sending lead ripping into the wagon, ricocheting off the big boulder, whining over the heads of the trembling horses.

"Enough!" Again the shooting stopped. Cowley called now, "We've got you outnumbered five to one."

Kirk said softly to Ira, "A few more barrages like that and there won't be any wagon left—or very much of us." He paused a moment and added in a whisper, "Jaw at Cowley for a while. Keep him talking."

He began to ease away, staying behind the sides of the wagon and working toward the front. Behind him Ira Moss called, "Which one of us you asking, Cowley?"

Cowley said, "All of you." Kirk slithered over the side of the wagon and dropped to the rock ledge alongside the wall.

"We got to take us a vote," Ira said. He sounded so believable that Kirk almost laughed aloud. He stifled it and began to slide along the ledge, working in the direction of the big rock.

"You've got two minutes."

"Give us five," Ira said. "We're all dug in different holes here."

Near Cowley, Weeb rumbled out a scornful laugh. "Rabbits!" he said. "You're wasting time, Lex. Open up on 'em again. That'll make up their minds fast enough."

"You see to the men," Cowley snapped. "I'll handle this."

Kirk stopped. He had reached the place where he wanted to be and no one seemed to have seen him. The wall threw a deep shadow here, cutting away the moonlight and forcing him to work by feel. He eased both hands forward until he touched the box of dynamite. He grunted in soft satisfaction.

A footstep scraped rock near him. Downes said out of the darkness, "Kirk?"

"That's right. And don't waste time asking me if Cowley would let us go. You know better."

"So do the women," Downes answered. "But if twenty-five men charge us—"

"In a few minutes, that's what I'll want them to do," Kirk said. He began to fuse a stick of dynamite.

Downes moved closer. "Let me give you a hand. I've done a little of this myself."

Kirk showed him by feel where the caps, the fuse, and the sticks were. Then he returned to work. Beyond them, the silence ticked away. Cowley called finally, "Your time is up."

Kirk said softly, "How many sticks do you have?"

111

"Four ready."

Kirk thrust two at him. "Here. That makes us six apiece. Go back to the rock and take the west slope. When I shout, throw the first one."

"Good God, man—without warning?"

"The first one will be warning enough," Kirk said. "I'm throwing it short. Try to hit the edge of the swamp at the bottom of the slope. If they don't get the message, throw one into them."

"Fair enough," Downes snapped.

Cowley cried, "Set your men, Weeb. Red, you ready over there?"

Kirk started back toward the wagon. "Give us another minute, Cowley. We've got a couple of stubborn females down here."

He could hear the mutter of voices as Weeb said something to Cowley and Cowley answered. Both voices were too low for Kirk to catch the words. Finally, Cowley said, "No more time."

Kirk stopped short of the wagon, crouched and laid down all but one stick of his dynamite. He was exposed here to both a direct shot or a ricochet. Quickly he struck a match and lit the short fuse on the dynamite. "Now, Marshall!"

A gun slammed immediately. The bullet struck the wall near Kirk's head, sending small rock shards whining against the side of his face. He rose to his full height and threw, sending the dynamite in a high arc. For a moment he thought he had sent it too high, that it would go off well before it hit the ground. But then it began to descend, trailing its tiny sputtering tail. The darkness of the swamp grass swallowed it.

The world seemed to erupt in one great surge of sound as dynamite exploded both to the west and to the east. Great gouts of mud and slime mixed with grass roots lifted into the air and rained down in all directions.

Two guns cracked from the west, one from the east. Then a voice came through the fading rumble of sound. "Dynamite, by God! I'm getting out of here!"

Kirk called, "There's plenty more where that came from. Now let's see a fire on each hill and a line of you empty-handed heros reaching for the sky. And make it fast!"

Weeb swore. "Shoot! Charge them, you fools!"

Kirk lit a second stick. "Again, Marshal!" Once more he threw, this time harder, with less arc. Just as he released the stick a gun cracked. He felt the bullet take him in the left arm, spinning him around. He slammed against the wall. For a moment he thought the force of his striking the rough rock had put the roaring into his ears. Then he realized the dynamite had gone off a quarter of the way up the slope.

Now rock and tree roots rained down along with the dry dirt of the hillside. Men's voices raised in fear and pain. Someone cried, "I'm blinded! Get me away from here!"

His words were cut off as another explosion came from the west slope. As that faded, Cowley could be heard shouting, "Pull to the top of the hill. We'll starve them out if it takes a month! Pull back."

Kirk lit a third stick and threw it as hard and far as he could, shouting his signal at the same time. He could feel the blood running down his left arm and trickling off his fingers, but the shock had not yet gone, so he felt no pain.

The third stick struck halfway up the hill, rolled a short distance and erupted. An explosion from the west slope followed. Kirk could see figures spurting into the moonlight; men on foot ran for cover and men on horseback sent their frightened animals racing to safety.

"All the way back!" Cowley shouted. "And keep shooting. Keep them off balance!"

Opie's shrill tones pierced the momentary silence that

followed Cowley's orders. "Someone's coming. A whole passel of riders heading this way."

Kirk cried, "That'll be the posse from town, Cowley. Where are you going to run to now?"

Cowley's wordless cry filled the night, and Kirk knew that the man's patience had snapped at last. Finally he choked out, "Ride! We'll take care of this later. Ride. You know where to go!"

Kirk turned and stumbled toward the big rock. He saw an outline of Mindy as she rose to take aim with her rifle. "Hold your fire," he said. "And lend me your horse. If Cowley gets away now, he'll come back with an army."

She said tersely, "Help yourself," and climbed down from the rock.

Kirk hurried to where Carla still held the horses. He located Mindy's horse, quickly lowered the stirrups and climbed into the tight saddle. The pain struck suddenly and he grabbed for leather to keep from falling.

Mindy was directly below him. "That's blood I felt. You've been hurt!"

"A scratch," Kirk said through clenched teeth. He felt like a fool. To keep her from arguing, he spurred the horse to the meadow and fought it through the muck to the west slope. Marshal Downes came tightly on his heels.

From beyond the rim of the slope guns began to crack. Opie could be heard crying, "The posse! Weeb? Where are you, Weeb?"

And then Cowley shouted, "Ride and scatter. Save your lead and ride!"

Kirk topped the rim of the slope and fought the horse through a thicket of small pines. To his right, toward the valley, a familiar voice called, "There goes Lex—and Weeb!"

A big, gold horse burst into view almost in front of Kirk. He said wonderingly, "Fancher! Arthur Fancher!"

Moonlight gleamed on Fancher's face, damp with a shine

of sweat. "Kirk! They rode toward the Oval-M." He heeled the gold and sent it thundering through the trees.

"You crazy fool," Kirk whispered. "They'll shoot you on sight!" He kicked Mindy's horse into action and followed, leaving Downes behind.

He could hear the gold ahead; the trail leading to the Oval-M was under his horse's hoofs. He could see some distance and he made out two riders at the edge of the clearing in front of Ira's house. Between him and them was Fancher, punishing the gold, forcing it to gain ground.

"Lex!" he cried. "Stand and fight, Lex!"

Cowley's big white horse stopped, pawing the air, and spun around. "Arthur," Cowley shouted, and laughed. Beside him, Weeb stopped, too. He turned his horse and Kirk saw a moonlight gleam on the barrel of his gun. Not slacking his pace, Kirk drew the fancy .44 he had taken from Cowley, lifted it and fired. Weeb jerked sideways and his shot went screaming into the night.

Kirk came alongside Fancher. "Leave Cowley to me. You don't want his blood on your hands."

Ahead, Cowley threw up a rifle and fired. The bullet took Kirk's horse in the chest, stopping it as if it had been pole-axed. He felt the sudden halt, kicked free of the stirrups and jumped as the horse began to go down. He landed on the rough trail, stumbled and caught himself.

Cowley fired again, catching Kirk along the edge of his hip, knocking him sprawling. Kirk rose to one knee, clench-ing his teeth against the welling pain from his bleeding thigh and arm. He saw Weeb riding straight for them, gun up and ready, and he saw Arthur Fancher stand in the stirrups and lift a gun awkwardly. He thrust it straight out in front of him.

Kirk saw Cowley wheel the white horse to get out of Weeb's line. Cowley lifted his rifle. "Arthur's mine!" he called thickly.

Kirk lifted his .44 and shot Cowley through the body. He lifted out of the saddle, slapped hard on the trail, rolled once and lay still. Weeb jerked his head and then swung back and shot at Fancher. Fancher's hat went winging away. Then he answered the shot. Kirk watched as Weeb threw up his arms, lost his gun and then slid slowly out of the saddle to land a few feet from Cowley. Fancher kept firing the gun convulsively until it was empty.

Kirk said, "It's all over, Arthur."

Fancher turned and the dazed look on his face began to clear. He said, "I got all the way to Portland before I realized that running wasn't the answer. So I started back; I bought a gun and practiced every day."

He rode near Kirk. "I'm still not very good," he said.

"Good enough," Kirk answered and pitched forward as darkness claimed him.

Kirk thought he smelled coffee and he wondered about it. His eyes came open and he stared into Mindy's anxious features. He said, "Are you all right?"

A smile lifted the corners of her full mouth. "It's about time you came around. Are you going to sleep forever?"

Kirk listened to the bubble of her laughter, knowing that it was relief for him. He said, "How long has it been?"

"Just yesterday. Doc Irmser patched you up late last night. He patched up the marshal, too. Opie shot him in the back. But it only grazed a rib. He's up and walking."

"And Arthur?"

"With Carla," Mindy said. "Six of Cowley's men are dead and three are wounded and in jail. The rest have scattered. There isn't a man who rode for Cowley still free in Snowy Valley."

Kirk closed his eyes and opened them again, feeling a weight lift from him. "How long does the Doc think I'll be here?" He looked around, seeing that he was back in his room at Mindy's.

"You'll be hobbling in a week," she said. "You can be back at the dam site in another week. Carla wants you to finish it."

He nodded. She said, "And then what will you do?"

"Ranch," he said. "If Arthur owns the L-in-C, maybe he'll sell me back the piece my father once owned."

"He's already agreed to that," she said. "Ira claims that the two places, that one and the Oval-M, together make a nice spread. He thinks they'll support all three of us."

Kirk lifted his head. "Three? Are you going ranching too?"

"I do what my man does," Mindy said softly. She bent and touched her lips to his. "But I think I'll hang on to this for a while—until you get on your feet and stock your range."

"I figure you're talking about getting married," Kirk said dryly.

"I waited long enough for you to ask," she answered. Her smile came again. "Does that make me shameless?"

He reached up and drew her to him. "I won't answer that just yet," he said. His mouth twitched in a smile. "Right now, I've got other things on my mind?"

He watched a puzzled expression slip over her features. He laughed softly. "Two things," he said. "Food—and kissing you."

She bent farther forward. "You can eat later," she whispered.

Louis Trimble was born in Seattle, Washington, and during most of his professional career taught in the University of Washington system of higher education. 'I began writing Western fiction,' he later observed, 'because of my interest in the history and physical character of the western United States and because the Western was (and is) a genre in which a writer could move with a great deal of freedom.' His first Western novel under the Louis Trimble byline was *Valley of Violence* (1948). In this and his subsequent Western novels he seems to have been most influenced by Ernest Haycox, another author who lived in the Pacific Northwest. He also used the *nom de plume* **Stuart Brock** under which he wrote five exceptional Westerns, all published by Avalon Books in the 1950s. The point of focus in his Western fiction, whether he is writing as Louis Trimble or Stuart Brock, constantly shifts among various viewpoints and women are often major characters. *Railtown Sheriff* (1949) was Trimble's first Western novel as Stuart Brock and it was under this byline that some of his most exceptional work appeared, most notably *Action at Boundary Peak* and *Whispering Canyon*, both in 1955, and *Forbidden Range* in 1956. These novels have strong characters, complex and realistic situations truly reflecting American life on the frontier, and often there is a mystery element that heightens a reader's interest. The terrain of the physical settings in these stories is vividly evoked and is an essential ingredient in the narrative. Following his retirement from academic work, Trimble made his retirement home in Devon, England.